Ride the Hot Wind

RIDE THE HOT WIND

LEWIS B. PATTEN

THORNDIKE
CHIVERS

LIBRARY OF CONGRESS CATALOGING-IN-PUBLICATION DATA

Patten, Lewis B.
  Ride the hot wind / by Lewis B. Patten.
    p. cm. — (Thorndike Press large print westerns)
  ISBN 0-7862-8984-8 (alk. paper)
  1. Large type books. I. Title.
PS3566.A79R53 2006
813'.54—dc22   2006019203

BRITISH LIBRARY CATALOGUING-IN-PUBLICATION DATA AVAILABLE

Published in 2006 in the U.S. by arrangement with Golden West Literary Agency.
Published in 2007 in the U.K. by arrangement with Golden West Literary Agency.

U.K. Hardcover: 978 1 405 63932 3 (Chivers Large Print)
U.K. Softcover: 978 1 405 63933 0 (Camden Large Print)

Printed in the United States of America on permanent paper.
10 9 8 7 6 5 4 3 2 1

RIDE THE HOT WIND

I

Frank Kilburn halted his horse briefly at the head of the narrow trail. It was two in the afternoon and the day's heat was at its worst. He shoved back his hat and mopped his forehead with his bandanna. He glanced at Glen Epperson, his prisoner. Epperson scowled at him and a faint irritability stirred in Kilburn's mind. Turning, he kneed his horse down the trail toward the rimrock, pulling Epperson's horse impatiently along behind.

A strong, hot wind blew up the canyon from the south, lifting dust clouds from the steep, denuded slopes below the rim. They swirled high on the hot, rising air and spreading, put a yellow halo around the sun. The valley floor, two thousand feet below, was nearly obscured by a haze of yellow dust, but Kilburn didn't have to see it to know it was brown, burned out by months of drought.

The sky wasn't even blue anymore, Kilburn thought. It was yellow like the dust. And although he hadn't seen a real cloud for weeks, there always were the clouds of dust, lifted high on the never-ending wind. And the heat, blistering everything it touched, seemed to grow worse with every passing day.

The fleeting thought crossed his mind that maybe everything was coming to an end. Maybe it wasn't ever going to rain again. Maybe nothing would ever grow. The cattle would die, and eventually the men would, too. Already every single water hole on the plateau top was dry. In two days of riding he hadn't seen a cow. Instead of being up where there still remained a little browning grass, the cattle were bunched in the valley along the creek, which was only a trickle now. They were starving because they no longer had the strength to walk back to where there still was something for them to eat.

Frank Kilburn was a tall, sunbaked man who looked about ten years older than he really was. His skin was brown and leathery and his eyes were blue, surrounded by wrinkles caused partly by good humor, partly by a lifetime of squinting against the glare. He rode slouched, relaxed and comfortable, his sweat-stained hat pulled low in front to shield his eyes. He wore a khaki shirt, sweat-stained beneath the armpits and down the back, faded blue Levis and scuffed, run down at the heel Texas boots. A silver star was pinned to the pocket of his shirt, bright not from polishing but from being worn. Kilburn was sheriff of Arroyo Blanco County. He was returning to Guthrie, the county seat, with Glen Epperson, his prisoner. Epperson, crazed with rage, had killed a man after a drunken fight two nights before by shooting him in the back; he would probably hang for it.

Kilburn carried no revolver, but a rifle stock protruded from a scuffed saddle boot beneath his right leg. The two horses picked their careful way down the trail to the place where it negotiated the precipitous sandstone rim. Here, Kilburn dismounted and led his horse. Epperson stayed in the saddle, since his hands were cuffed behind his back, but he swung his left leg over to the right side of his saddle so that it wouldn't scrape against the wall of rock. As soon as they were through the rim Kilburn swung into his saddle again.

At the foot of the steep, bare slide they entered a forest of cedars and piñon pine. Even these were turning brown. The horses' hooves stirred dust that was instantly whipped away by the hot south wind.

Kilburn dreaded returning to the county seat. Being sheriff these days was like sitting on a powder keg. The Guthrie bank had already called several cattle and first mortgage loans. From one end of Red Creek to the other men were desperate, watching their life's work dissipate as their starving cattle died. That was bad enough. But to make it worse, Adam Guthrie had several thousand acres of grass hay land on which the hay was too short to cut. He also had several hundred tons of hay in stacks that had been carried over from years gone by. He had refused to sell either the pasture or the hay, saying he needed both himself.

Guthrie's was a hell of a selfish attitude, Kilburn thought, but he couldn't argue with the man's right to keep his own cattle from dying if he could. Still, he knew that Guthrie was taking an awful chance. The whole country was teetering on the brink of violence. If it eruped, Guthrie would probably be its first victim. Despite his money and his cattle and his thousands of acres of land, both in the valley and on top of the plateau, Guthrie could be wiped out along with the rest of the country's inhabitants. It was Kilburn's thankless job to see that nobody did anything he would later be sorry for.

He reached the road and glanced around at his prisoner again. Epperson was a bachelor, one of the smaller ranchers on Red Creek. He had never been in trouble with the law before, and Kilburn knew that he wouldn't be now if he hadn't first been driven to despair by the heat, by being forced to watch helplessly while his cattle died, by being told the day before the fight that he was being foreclosed on by the Guthrie bank.

That didn't excuse killing a man, particularly by shooting him in the back. But if it hadn't been for this damned drought, Epperson wouldn't have killed anyone. He asked suddenly, "Want a drink?" in a voice he tried to make friendly in spite of the heat, in spite of his own weariness and growing sense of helplessness and irritability.

Epperson nodded, growling, "If there's still any water in the goddamn creek."

Kilburn led the way toward the creek through the high sagebrush, the leaves of which had been stripped from the branches as high as a cow could reach. The creek held a trickle of water less than two feet wide. He stepped wearily from his horse. Epperson dismounted by lifting his right leg over

11

the saddle horn and sliding to the ground.

Kilburn unlocked one of his wrists and relocked it again in front. Epperson lay on his stomach and drank. Glancing upstream, Kilburn saw two gaunt cows staring at him through the sagebrush. He could count every one of their ribs, and their hip bones protruded enough for him to have hung his hat on them.

Epperson got up, wiping his mouth with the back of his hand. He looked at the cattle and said, "I guess it hadn't ought to mean anything to me. I'm going to jail and the bank will get my cattle anyway. But I hate to see 'em look like that. It's a damn shame, that's what it is. If that sonofabitch Guthrie would let loose of some of the feed he's got . . ."

Kilburn said, "He's got cattle, too. You can't expect him to take feed from his own cattle so's he can give it to someone else."

Epperson didn't say anything. Kilburn walked upstream for a dozen yards, then lay down and drank himself. He got up, wiped his mouth and said, "All right, let's go."

Epperson mounted, leaving the reins dragging on the ground. Kilburn picked them up, mounted his own horse and led out toward the road. Epperson said plaintively, "Jesus Christ, it's hot!"

12

Kilburn began to think about the cold beer he'd have after he had locked Epperson in the jail. He licked his lips, which were dry and cracked. The two horses plodded down the road.

At six, when the pair entered the town of Guthrie, the sun was still well up in the western sky. Kilburn rode along the deserted street straight to the jail. He dismounted and tied both horses to the rail. Epperson slid down and stood waiting with a certain fatalism. Kilburn said, "One good thing. The jail is cool."

Epperson nodded. Kilburn opened the door and waited for his prisoner to go inside. Epperson went into the jail's only cell, and Kilburn closed and locked the door. "Anything special you want to eat?"

Epperson shook his head. "But I *would* like a beer."

Kilburn started to refuse, then stopped. He wasn't supposed to serve beer to prisoners, but to hell with that. He said, "Sure," then went out, locking the stout plank door behind him.

There was only one saloon in town. It was called the Ute Saloon, and there was a weathered wooden Indian standing on the sidewalk beside the door. Kilburn stepped inside.

Only half a dozen men were here. Two were cowhands employed by Adam Guthrie. A third was Hugo Enzbarger, bearded and gray and thick bodied, staring sourly at the schooner of beer in front of him. Oscar Tafoya, the sheepman, was the fourth, and two of his three sons were with him. Ute Willis, who owned the saloon, was behind the bar. He drew a beer without being told and slid it to Kilburn, who picked it up and took a long slow drink.

Wiping foam from his mouth, he looked at Tafoya. "How are the sheep making it?"

Tafoya shrugged almost imperceptibly. "Better than cattle. We can keep them on the mountain and bring them off every couple of days to drink. We'll make it if the drought don't last too long."

Enzbarger butted in, "And you take every damn bit of feed within walkin' distance of the creek. No wonder the cattle are starvin' to death."

Tafoya said, "The cattle wouldn't walk to it anyway."

Enzbarger glared at him. "They would if it wasn't so goddamn far away."

Kilburn said, "All right, let's don't start anything."

Enzbarger said, "That bastard Mex. We shoulda drove him out when he first came

14

here with them goddamn sheep."

Kilburn said, "Shut up, Hugo."

"Who you telling to shut up? Who the hell do you think you are, anyway?"

"You know who I am. Now stop it or go on home."

"Why don't you tell that goddamn Mex to leave?"

"Because he's not making the trouble. You are."

Tafoya interrupted softly, "It's all right, Sheriff. We'll go."

The eldest of his sons was flushed. His eyes were angry. "Why? Why will we go? We got just as much right to be here as that . . . as he has."

Tafoya said sharply, "Joseph!"

Joseph would not be silenced. "Why have we got to go?" he insisted. "Why?"

Tafoya said, "To avoid trouble."

"Avoid trouble? You can't avoid trouble by running away from it."

"That's enough."

Kilburn said, "If anybody's going anyplace, it's going to be Mr. Enzbarger. Now, for God's sake, let's let it drop."

Enzbarger's face was dark. He was sweating heavily. He gulped his beer and stalked to the door, muttering beneath his breath. Kilburn said, "It's the heat. And watching the cattle die. And not being able to do anything."

Tafoya asked, "Did you catch Epperson?"

"Uh huh. He's down at the jail." He lifted his beer mug and drained it. He said, "Give me another, Ute, for Glen. I'll bring the mug back later."

Ute drew another beer. Kilburn left two nickels on the bar and carried the schooner out into the street. There was a thermometer beside the door where the sun didn't hit it and he looked at it. It registered 107°.

No wonder tempers were short, he thought. Even at night it rarely dropped below ninety. And there was always that damned wind, drying things out, blowing away the land. A man's mouth always had grit in it. There was dust in the food, dust on everything he touched.

He glanced at the Guthrie bank. Its doors were closed and its blinds were drawn.

He guessed he couldn't blame the trouble entirely on the bank. The bank had more to lose than anyone. But he didn't understand how they expected to gain by foreclosing mortgages, by seizing cattle to settle overdue cattle loans. There was no market for the ranches they foreclosed. The cattle were seized, wouldn't bring much more than the value of their hides.

16

He unlocked the jail door and carried the mug of beer inside. Epperson took it when he passed it between the bars. He took a long drink and wiped his mouth on his sleeve. He said feelingly, "Thanks, Frank."

"Sure. I'm going to eat. I'll bring your supper back with me."

Epperson nodded. Holding the beer, he went over and sat down on the cot.

Kilburn went out the door. The heat had not abated. Feeling touchy and irritable, he crossed the street diagonally toward the restaurant.

II

The town of Guthrie had eighty-seven inhabitants. It had two principal streets, at right angles to each other. One terminated on the western end at the railroad depot. Becoming a road, it ran east along the river toward the town of Ibid, twenty miles away.

The other ran north along Red Creek until it petered out in thick brush and down timber nearly fifty miles from town. Southward, it wound across the flats on the other side of the river and then followed the river in a southwesterly direction toward Junction City, fifty miles away.

The north-south street was called First Street, and the other was called Main. The Guthrie bank, built of sandstone blocks, stood on the northeast corner of the intersection. Diagonally across from it was the Guthrie Hotel: frame, two stories high, and painted pale yellow. A second story balcony ran the length and width of the hotel, and below, at street level, was a veranda, facing Main, upon which there were a number of rocking chairs, usually occupied by the town's older male residents.

On the southeast corner was Maggie Morgan's restaurant and diagonally across from that was the drugstore. Next to the drugstore was a saddle and a gun shop, and next to that the Ute Saloon. Beyond the saloon was Littlejohn's Mercantile, with a lumberyard adjoining on the west, a furniture store on the east. Down beyond the depot was Littlejohn's sawmill, which got its logs by rail from the high country a hundred miles east of town. The mill only operated about one day a week and was driven by a big steam engine fueled by the sawmill's slabs. Between the depot and the main part of town was the sandstone block jail and the Guthrie Livery Stable, a towering, green frame structure that was beginning to sag and lean. When the wind blew extra strong, its creaking could be heard all over town, but nobody seemed to consider seriously the possibility that it might one day collapse.

Inside of the restaurant, it was even hotter than it was outside. Kilburn sat down at the counter and put his hat on the stool next to him.

Jennie Morgan, Maggie's daughter, came from the kitchen, brushing a damp wisp of dark hair from her forehead with the back of a hand. She was obviously tired, obviously suffering from the heat, but she gave Kilburn a warm smile. He had been taking Jennie to dances at the Odd Fellow's Hall for a long time and, if he had been asked directly, would have admitted, after some frowning hesitation, that he would probably marry her someday, if she'd have him, which he doubted because what girl would want a bachelor in his middle thirties. It had never occured to him that Jennie herself was thirty or that she might, sometimes, feel desperate.

She asked, "Did you get Glen Epperson?"

He nodded.

Jennie looked relieved. "Did he put up a fight?"

Kilburn shook his head. "He thought

about it, but he changed his mind."

"I'll bet you're hungry. What do you want to eat?"

"Do I smell chicken?"

"And dumplings. Want some of that?"

"Uh huh. And something cold."

"I've got some cold lemonade. This is about the last of the ice, though. It took me ten minutes to find a chunk last time I went to the ice house, and it wasn't much bigger than fifteen pounds."

Kilburn said, "That will be fine." If Jennie's ice was gone, then Ute Willis's ice must be almost gone too. That would mean warm beer, and warm beer wouldn't help dispositions already frayed by heat and dust and uncertainty.

Jennie looked at Kilburn's face for a moment, seeing the weariness, the frustration and irritability and understanding it. Then she turned and disappeared into the kitchen. He heard her talking to her mother, but he couldn't make out their words. A few moments later, Maggie Morgan came from the kitchen, a glass of lemonade in her hand. A single piece of ice clinked pleasantly in it.

She put it down in front of him. "You look tired."

"I am. I didn't dare sleep much last night. I didn't think Glen would try anything, but

I couldn't be too sure."

She said, "There were three fights in the saloon last night. And one in here."

He said, "I wish it would cloud up and rain."

"It won't."

"How do you know that?"

"I saw a spell like this back home when I was a little girl. It didn't rain all summer. And it didn't snow that winter, either."

"But the people survived."

"Yes. But that wasn't cattle country. The problems weren't the same. And there wasn't any Adam Guthrie playing dog-in-the-manger with his feed."

"Or a bank foreclosing mortgages."

"No. At least I don't remember anything like that."

Maggie brought his food. She retired immediately to the kitchen. Jennie got a glass of lemonade for herself and came around the counter to sit beside him. Kilburn began to eat. Between bites he asked, "How are you and your mother making it? With nobody having any money, I don't suppose your business is too good."

She shook her head. "No. But we don't owe the bank anything. And we don't need much."

There was a moment's silence. Finally she

21

asked, "What's going to happen to Glen?"

Kilburn frowned. "He'll probably hang." He turned his head and stared out the window. The wind had lessened with the ending of the day but it still had force enough to stir a dust cloud in the street in front of the restaurant. He looked along Main toward the eastern edge of town, toward the white courthouse with its bell cupola. There was a church across the street from it, and the two buildings looked much the same. He saw Judge Barngrover come down the courthouse steps carrying his coat and hat and turn toward home. He asked, "Have they buried Miller Gross yet?"

"Today."

"Any trouble at the funeral?"

She shook her head. "The Red Creek ranchers stood on one side of the grave and Adam Guthrie's men stood on the other. They just glared at each other, and afterward the Red Creek ranchers went to the saloon. Mr. Guthrie took his men home with him."

Miller Gross had been one of Adam Guthrie's hands, and the killing had intensified the animosity already existing between Guthrie and his men and the other ranchers along Red Creek. There may not have been trouble at the funeral but the trial would be something else. And if Glen Epperson should be sentenced to hang . . . He shook his head. He didn't want to think of that.

Maybe he could get Judge Barngrover to postpone the trial. If it could be put off until after it had rained . . . But he didn't suppose it could. Nobody had the slightest idea when it was going to rain.

He finished eating and drank the last of his lemonade. He asked, "Mind fixing a plate for Glen?"

Jennie got up and went around the counter into the kitchen. Kilburn realized that he was soaked. Just eating had been exertion enough to make him break out in a sweat. He rubbed his stubbled face ruefully, wishing he'd taken time to clean up and shave before coming here to eat.

Jennie returned with a tray covered with a bleached white flour sack dish towel. He could hear the clink of a piece of ice in a glass of lemonade underneath. He paid for both meals, then carried the tray out into the street while Jennie held the door. She called after him, "Come by later if you feel like it. After it cools off."

Kilburn carried the tray across the intersection and along the street. Two men were waiting in front of the jail. One was Ross

Lockhart, a neighbor of Epperson's, and the other was Tako Nomura, his hired man. Kilburn knew Lockhart hadn't paid Nomura any wages for months. Nomura stayed, for his keep, because he didn't know where else to go. Lockhart was sweating and he looked edgy. "I hear you brought Glen in."

Kilburn nodded, watching Lockhart warily.

"Well, can we see him?"

"I guess you can." He handed the tray to Nomura, a tiny, bowlegged Japanese who spoke no more English than was absolutely necessary to get by. Looking at Lockhart he said, "Give me your gun."

Lockhart scowled. "Why, for Christ's sake? You think I'm going to try breaking him out of jail?"

Kilburn asked irritably, "Do you want to see him or not?"

"You don't have to be so damn hard nosed about it."

Kilburn took the gun Lockhart handed him and stuck it into his belt. He said, "I've been out two days, and last night I didn't get any sleep. The heat's getting me just like it is you." He unlocked the door, took the tray from Nomura and let the two go in ahead of him. They waited while he crossed the room and slid the tray under the barred cell door.

He came back and sat down at his desk. Nomura stayed back, but Lockhart went to the bars. "How you doin', Glen?"

Epperson shrugged. "All right, I guess."

"Cool in here anyway, ain't it?"

"Better'n out in the sun, I guess, but I ain't never been locked up before. It gives me a crazy feeling in the head. I feel like tearin' these bars out with my bare hands, or yellin' or something. Or maybe just cryin' like I did when I was a kid."

"You ain't going to be in here very long."

Epperson stared at him. "You crazy or something? I ain't never going to get out. Not until they take me out to hang me anyways."

"It was a fight. They don't hang a man for killin' somebody in a fight."

"They do for shootin' somebody in the back. An' that's what I did. Maybe a dozen men saw me shoot Miller Gross."

Lockhart said, "You got friends."

Epperson seemed to lose interest in Lockhart. He said, "I'm hungry. Thanks for coming, Ross."

"Sure." Lockhart got his gun from Kilburn and went out. Nomura followed him silently. Kilburn closed the door against the

25

heat radiating in from the street. Epperson was sitting on his bunk, the tray on his lap. Kilburn heard the ice clink inside the glass.

After a while, Epperson asked, "*You* think I got any chance of ever walking out of here?"

"I wouldn't get my hopes up if I were you. Still, juries do funny things."

Epperson finished eating. "I gotta go to the outhouse."

"All right. Slide the tray under the door."

Epperson slid the tray out. Kilburn picked it up and put it on the desk. He took a revolver out of a desk drawer and stuck it into his belt. He unlocked the cell door and followed Epperson out into the street. Epperson took the well-worn path leading to the rear of the jail where the outhouse was. Kilburn waited until he came out again, then followed him back into the jail. He locked him in the cell again, picked up the tray and went back outside, once more carefully locking the door behind him. Some of the smaller Red Creek ranchers were pretty desperate, and he knew they were capable of trying to break Epperson out of jail.

He picked up the tray. As he walked toward the restaurant, he glanced up at the sky. The sun was just going down behind the high mesa west of town. The shadow of the mesa raced swiftly across town from west to east. The sky was still full of dust, despite the lessened wind. And the heat stayed in the street, seeming to be trapped. It radiated up from the sandstone slab sidewalk and from the deep dust in the middle of the street.

There were a few trees in town, but their leaves were turning brown. Passing the bank, looking at its dark green, drawn blinds, Kilburn wondered why foreclosing people's ranches and cattle made sense to Nelson Struthers, president of the bank. It looked like it would be better business to give people a chance to get back on their feet and repay their loans.

And then he suddenly got to wondering if Nelson Struthers really owned the bank, owned all of it the way everybody assumed he did. If, for instance, Adam Guthrie owned part of it, then maybe the foreclosing would make some sense.

Kilburn shook his head and crossed the street to the restaurant. The heat was getting him. Guthrie didn't own the bank. And even if he did, he wouldn't close out his neighbors just to get their cattle and their land.

But he was still frowning slightly as he went into the restaurant, and the suspicion that had just been born in his mind did not immediately go away.

III

At the head of Red Creek the vegetation was different than it was at the lower altitudes near Guthrie. There was no greasewood and the sagebrush was short, no higher than a couple of feet at most. There was serviceberry brush and scrub oak, but leaves had been eaten off the brush by sheep and by cattle until, despite the altitude, the land was like a desert.

In a wide draw called Trail Gulch, sheep were like a gray undulating tide. Behind them rode a man, Domingo Tafoya, youngest son of Oscar Tafoya, who had been left in charge while his father and two older brothers drove the wagon to Guthrie for supplies. He was a dark-faced, slightly built young man, nineteen on his last birthday. He lounged comfortably in his saddle, hat pulled low in front to shield his eyes from the hot glare of the sun. Ahead of him and spread across the draw were the sheep, four thousand of them in all. Working the flanks of the flock were the two dogs, Shep and Gray.

The tide of sheep flowed slowly toward Red Creek. Occasionally a bell, hung around one's neck, would tinkle as an animal raised its head. They picked at the few browning leaves still clinging to the brush. They found an occasional nip of grass where there seemed to be nothing but barren ground. When the wind shifted and brought the smell of the water in the creek to them, they gave up their desultory feeding and moved more briskly toward it. Domingo and the two dogs ranged back and forth, urging on the stragglers.

Dust raised by the sheep became stifling. It lifted in a cloud and all but blotted out the setting sun. And combining with the dust was the stench of the sheep themselves, which Domingo never had got used to, no matter how much he was exposed to it.

He was hot and tired, and he was irritable because he had wanted to go to town. Besides that, he hated sheep. He hated their smell and their idiotic bleating and their stupidity. Most of all, he hated them because they made him an outcast, shunned by the other people of the community.

He shook his head now with rueful honesty, admitting that it wasn't altogether because of the sheep that he, his father and brothers were outcasts. It was also because they were Mexicans. And maybe because they were more fortunate than the cattle-men. They could drive their sheep up onto the plateau to graze. They could water them every couple of days in the creek. The sheep would lose weight from so much traveling, but they would not starve and die as the cattle would.

He rode his horse up onto a small knoll at one side of the draw. From his vantage point he could see the valley of Red Creek for about half a mile above and below the place at which the sheep would cross the road. Near the creek he could see the covered wagon which served him, his father and brothers as a home. The first of the sheep were just beginning to cross the road.

Suddenly he stiffened. Below the point where the sheep were crossing he saw something else. Three riders were coming up the road.

He recognized them instantly. They were the three sons of Hugo Enzbarger: Rudy, Karl and Sam.

The sheep had filled the road. And still they came, crowding, bleating, but slowed almost to a stop by those ahead, halted and drinking out of the creek.

The three Enzbargers spurred their horses, trying to push through the mass of wooly bodies. The sheep bleated, but they could not get out of the way. They were packed too tightly, blocked from going on, blocked from going back. Domingo heard the Enzbargers shouting and knew they were cursing both the sheep and the Mexicans who owned them.

A strange feeling of emptiness came to his belly. His heart beat faster and his knees began to shake. He hated to admit it but he was afraid of these three big, dirty, hairy men. He kicked his horse into a lope so that he could clear the road for them, and he called the dogs.

While he was still three hundred yards away, galloping through serviceberry brush higher than his head, he heard their guns begin to bark. Then, suddenly, he was out of the brush, and he could see that they were not just shooting into the air.

They were firing directly into the flock, and the roaring of their guns had thoroughly terrified the sheep. Those nearest the creek literally climbed upon the backs of these below the road. Those above the road turned back, pushing frantically against the pressure of those coming up behind.

Slowly, a narrow passageway opened up, lengthening as the three Enzbarger brothers rode their plunging mounts into it. They continued to shoot, not over the heads of the sheep, but directly into those still blocking their way.

Domingo reached the edge of the flock behind the three. Several sheep were lying in the road, blood staining their dirty wool. He shouted furiously at the Enzbargers, "Hey, by God! You stop shooting sheep! You sonsabitches, you got to pay us for them sheep!"

The three men stopped. Karl was the oldest of the three. He was near thirty, bearded, hairy-chested and grossly fat, wearing a thin, sweat-stained shirt and filthy woolen pants he had made shiny in front by wiping his greasy hands on them. He wore a black felt hat pulled low over an unruly shock of prematurely graying hair. His eyes were like his father's: mean and small and close set, but startlingly blue.

Sam was the second, and he must have been about five years younger than Karl. He was neither as hulking nor as fat. He hadn't shaved for days, but he wore no beard as such. Like Karl, he had the Enzbarger eyes, but his mouth was fuller than his brother's, his lips chapped and tobacco stained.

Rudy, the youngest, was about Domingo's age, but taller and heavier than Domingo was. He wore a fancy black leather vest and black leather boots to match. His spurs were silver mounted and had big Spanish cartwheel rowels on them. The three turned their horses and sat in the road abreast, scowling at Domingo. Like Domingo, they were hot and irritable, and he suddenly offered them an object upon which to vent their spleen.

He rode to within ten feet of them. The sheep had crowded on up the road, leaving the area around the Enzbargers clear. Seven sheep lay dead and an eighth was kicking, bleating piteously all the while. There must be others wounded, Domingo thought, and some of those would die.

He felt sick at his stomach. How was he going to explain this to his father? He had been left in charge and this had happened. He was responsible.

He was afraid, but in the face of his outrage and perhaps goaded on by the heat, he began to curse the three men who sat there glowering at him as if he was the one who was in the wrong. So furious was he that he didn't pay any particular attention when Sam began to edge his horse away to the right and Rudy to the left.

Sam, on the uphill side of the road, suddenly yelled at him. He glanced that way, startled. Catching movement on the down-hill side of the road out of the corner of his eye, he jerked his head back in time to see the loop of Rudy's rope sailing toward him.

He tried to duck, tried to raise his hands and ward it off. But he was too late. The loop settled over his head and Rudy jerked it tight. Then, howling gleefully, he dallied it and sank spurs into his horse's sides.

With a vicious jerk, Domingo was yanked from his saddle. He struck the road with a thump that knocked the wind out of him. Stunned, he had the feeling of violent motion, of blows and jerks, and of the rope cutting cruelly into his arms and chest and back. There was dirt in his eyes and in his nose and mouth. There was a burning sensation as skin was scraped away on brush or on the rocky ground.

He was angrier than he had ever been before, but he was more helpless, too. And he was terrified because he knew that whether he lived or died depended entirely on how long Rudy Enzbarger continued this savage game.

Like everyone else, the Enzbarger brothers were victims of the heat, the dust, the drought. They had been riding the creek bottom, and the sight of dead and dying cattle had created in all three a helpless feeling of frustration. To be blocked by sheep, hated by all of them, had triggered a kind of explosion in their minds.

Rudy had started the shooting. When he yanked out his gun, he had intended only to shoot over their heads, frighten them, open a way through the press of stinking, wooly bodies. But he hadn't fired over their heads. He had fired into them and had felt a kind of fierce elation when he saw them go down and lie still in the dusty road.

His brothers had immediately drawn their own guns and started shooting also. And, slowly, a way had begun to open up.

None of the three had considered the certainty that one of the Tafoyas would be close by. Now, as Rudy heard the pound of a horse's hooves, he swung around, his revolver smoking and empty in his hand. His brothers followed suit, and the three sat there abreast watching Domingo Tafoya gallop toward them.

Domingo was furious, but Rudy could see that he was also scared. He glanced beyond Domingo, wondering where his father and brothers were. They did not appear. Domingo reined up his horse and began to yell something about them having to pay him for all the sheep that they had killed.

There was a rifle in a saddle boot beneath Domingo Tafoya's leg that he carried for coyotes and wolves and other predators. He seemed to have forgotten it.

Rudy tried not to look at it, but he couldn't get it off his mind. His own gun was empty, and he supposed his brothers' guns were empty, too. All three had stopped carrying rifles because there wasn't anything to hunt anymore. The deer were as scrawny as the cattle were.

Tafoya was obviously too angry right now to think about his gun. But if he ever did think of it . . . Rudy glanced at Sam. He could see that Sam, too, was thinking about the rifle. He gestured with his head and Sam edged away, leaving Karl in the middle of the road. Rudy edged away in the opposite direction.

Slowly and carefully so as not to attract Domingo's attention, Rudy took down his rope. He swiftly shook out a loop.

Tafoya turned. Rudy swung the loop and let it go. It settled over Tafoya's head. Rudy yanked the loop tight, pinning Tafoya's arms to his sides. He dallied the rope and spurred his horse. He felt the rope go taut then slacken as Tafoya hit the ground. He heard himself yelling exultantly as he continued to rake the horse's sweaty sides with the spurs.

The animal ran, veering away from the edge of the flock of sheep and streaking up the draw through the heavy brush.

Tafoya bounded and jerked along behind the horse like a limp rag doll. Grinning, Rudy whirled his horse and galloped back, Tafoya still alternately slackening and tightening the rope. He hauled his horse to a stop in front of his brothers. Karl now had Tafoya's rifle. Rudy said, "By God, that ought to hold him for a while, the Mexican sonofabitch." He swung to the ground and walked to where Tafoya lay.

Stooping, he took off the loop. He stirred Tafoya with his toe. "All right, Mex. You can get up now. But next time be careful who you give a cussin' to."

Domingo Tafoya didn't move. Rudy kicked him, saying in a voice suddenly shrill, "Hey, Mex! I said you could get up."

His mind refused to acknowledge what his eyes saw. There was no movement in Domingo Tafoya's chest. Rudy turned his head and looked first at Karl and then at Sam. There was panic in his eyes. He turned back to Tafoya and kicked him harder, shrilling at him, "Damn you, get up. Don't lay there like a stinkin' yellow dog!"

He heard a growl and looked toward the sound. One of the sheep dogs was crouching beside a clump of brush just above the road. His ears were laid back and his teeth were bared.

Sam said, in a shocked and awestruck voice, "Holy Christ, he's dead. He's really dead!"

The word put a chill of terror into Rudy's heart. He shouted, "You're a liar! He ain't dead; he's playin' possum!" But he knew that what Sam had said was true. Domingo Tafoya was dead!

But how? Dragging a man a little bit hadn't ought to kill him. He glanced back at Tafoya, lying at the edge of the road. Tafoya was covered with fine yellow dust, and his clothes were torn. Skin had been scraped off his face, and blood had combined with dust to put scabs of mud over the wounds. His hat had been lost somewhere, and his hair was full of dust. But there, at the side of his head, was a caved-in place, and blood ran darkly out to form a glistening pool on the dusty ground. Somehow or other, Tafoya's head had struck a rock while he was being dragged in just such a way as to split his skull.

Rudy looked up at his brothers, centering his glance on Karl. "What am I goin' to do? What the hell am I goin' to do?"

Karl threw Tafoya's rifle to the ground.

He said, "Get on your horse and come on home. Maybe we can figure somethin' out."

In spite of the heat, Rudy suddenly felt cold. The sweat on his skin felt clammy, and he was shivering. He climbed shakily onto his horse and coiled his rope automatically.

Karl led out and Rudy followed him. Sam brought up the rear, looking back uneasily every few moments as though expecting to be pursued. Rudy thought, "Oh my God, what am I goin' to say to Pa?"

IV

It was a little cooler with the sun down but not very much. There was still a residue of the sun's heat in the dust of the street and in the building walls. But the wind usually began to die after the sun set, and tonight was no exception to that rule.

Frank Kilburn paused a moment in front of the restaurant and glanced down the street. Oscar Tafoya and his two sons were loading their wagon in front of Littlejohn's Mercantile. Kilburn remembered hearing someone say once that Tafoya's mother had been German, hence the name Oscar. But that didn't seem to make any difference to the people around Guthrie. As far as they were concerned, Tafoya was all Mexican. Wryly Kilburn thought that if Tafoya had raised cattle instead of sheep he might have been able to overcome the stigma of being Mexican. He would never overcome the stigma of being a sheepman in a country of cattlemen.

Hugo Enzbarger came out of the saloon. He stopped on the walk and glanced up and down the street. He scowled at the Tafoyas, then untied his horse and mounted heavily. He trotted the horse up the street to the intersection and turned north up the Red Creek road.

He sat his horse like a lump of clay, heavily, putting no weight on the stirrups. Watching him, Kilburn thought uneasily that sooner or later there was going to be trouble between Enzbarger and the Tafoyas. They were neighbors at the head of the creek, and they competed for the same grass and water. Kilburn knew that when sheep compete with cattle, it is always the cattle that lose out. Sheep crop grass so close that cattle starve, and cattle will seldom drink where sheep have been.

He carried the tray into the restaurant and put it down on the end of the counter. There were three pople in the place, one of Guthrie's hired hands and a townsman and his wife. Kilburn nodded courteously at them.

Jennie came from the kitchen, having heard the door. Kilburn said, "I'm going over to the hotel and clean up. What time will you be closing?"

"Around eight, I suppose."

"I'll come by and walk you home."

"All right." She looked pleased. She raised a hand and brushed a damp wisp of hair away from her face.

He studied her, a half-smile on his mouth. Her hair was a rich, dark brown and matched her eyes. Her skin was smooth, a little flushed now from heat. Her mouth was full, and even when she was serious she gave the impression that she was just about to smile.

She felt his regard now and asked, "Have I got soot on my nose?"

He grinned. "Huh uh. I just like to look at you."

"You get out of here. I've got work to do."

Still grinning, he went to the door and stepped out into the street. He paused in front of the restaurant for a moment, taking time to pack and light his pipe. He wished he could quiet his uneasiness. He'd felt it ever since he got back to town with Epperson.

His horse and Epperson's were still tied in front of the jail. He crossed the street and untied them, then led them down to the livery barn. Inside, he yelled for the hostler. Tonight it was a gangling, yellow-haired boy of fifteen named Phil Whatley. Kilburn said, "They've been used pretty hard the last two days. Rub them down and give them each some oats. Not too much water, though."

"Yes sir, Sheriff. I'll take good care of them."

Kilburn turned and went back out into the street. His weariness hit him now, and his shoulders slumped. He wished he hadn't said anything to Jennie about walking her home. He'd like to get his bath and go to bed.

He tramped along the street to the corner and climbed the steps to the hotel veranda. Now that the sun was down, the usual collection of oldsters was there, smoking and swapping yarns. One called, "Have any trouble with Epperson?"

Kilburn shook his head and stepped into the lobby of the hotel.

It was the coolest place he had been today. Its ceiling was fourteen feet high. Stairs led up to the second floor.

Kilburn crossed the white tile floor without even glancing at the desk. His room was down the hall from the head of the stairs, and it faced east onto First Street.

He closed the door, crossed the room, raised the shade and then the window. He decided it was a toss-up whether it was hotter outside or inside the room.

He got himself a towel and clean clothes, then walked down the hall to the bathroom. There was a windmill on top of the hotel, and a wooden tank. The water, pumped up into the tank by the windmill, was gravity-fed through an iron pipe to bathrooms on the first and second floors.

Kilburn closed the door and began to fill the tub. There was no hot water and he wanted none. He peeled off his dusty, sweaty clothes and crawled into the tub. Cool for the first time that day, he lay back and closed his eyes for several moments before he began to scrub himself.

Twenty minutes later he got out of the tub and let the water drain. He dressed and carried his dirty clothes back to his room. He filled a pan from the white pitcher on the dresser and, after lathering, began to shave. Halfway through, he had to light the lamp.

It was fully dark by the time he had finished. He combed his hair, packed and lighted his pipe and blew out the lamp. Then he went out, descended the stairs and crossed the lobby to the street. At the jail, he unlocked the door, lighted a lamp and set it on the desk. Epperson was asleep and Kilburn didn't waken him. He stared for a moment at his holstered gun and cartridge belt hanging on a nail beside the door, then crossed to it, took it down and belted it around his waist. It felt strange and heavy there. He hadn't worn it more than once or twice in the last three years.

He wondered why he had put it on to-night. That strange feeling of uneasiness accounted for it, he supposed. As if he expected violence. As if he expected others to behave the way Epperson had three nights ago.

There were lamps burning in the restaurant, but no customers. Kilburn paused a moment to knock out his pipe on the heel of his boot. Straightening, he glanced down the alley behind the bank.

The alley was full of shadows, and there was very little light. But one of the shadows moved, and Kilburn stiffened automatically. Suddenly he was glad he had worn his gun tonight. He crossed the street at a run, dragging out the gun as he did. He plunged into the alley mouth unthinkingly, as if he did this every night.

He caught the movement again and yelled, "Hold it right where you are! I've got a gun, and I'll shoot if you force me to!"

The movement ceased. Realizing he was outlined against the light from the windows of the restaurant, Kilburn plunged across the alley and flattened himself against the wall of the bank. He said, "Come on out. Hands in the air."

Now he caught the movement again and heard a boot scrape against the hard-packed alley dirt. A man materialized out of the darkness, hands held in the air. Kilburn said, "Keep going out into the street so I can see who you are."

"Hell, I'll tell you that. It's Ross. Ross Lockhart."

"Anybody with you?"

"Huh uh."

"What are you doing here?"

"Is there some law that says a man can't walk down an alley?"

"You didn't answer my question."

"I had to . . . well hell, I been drinkin' beer."

"There's an outhouse behind the saloon."

"Sure there is, but this was handier."

Kilburn stared at Lockhart. He didn't really believe Ross's story, but he had no solid grounds for disbelieving it. He said, "All right, go on."

Lockhart shuffled away. Kilburn stared after him, frowning. He had a feeling Lockhart had been trying to get into the bank. He watched until Lockhart disappeared into the saloon. Then he turned and went into the restaurant.

Jennie was waiting for him. Her face was shiny from being washed and her hair was freshly combed. She blew out the lamps one by one, then came out and closed and locked the door behind her.

They turned away from the restaurant toward Jennie's house at the west end of town. She said, "Let's walk down by the creek. Maybe it will be cooler there."

Kilburn nodded. They walked in silence past the saloon, past Littlejohn's Mercantile, past the depot and finally past Littlejohn's sawmill with its towering pile of sawdust and slabs. The creek was beyond, and they descended the brushy bank, hearing its faint and pleasant sound as it trickled over the rocks.

Jennie Morgan guessed she felt as edgy as everyone else in town did tonight. The restaurant had been beastly hot all day, and it had been impossible to cool off even for a moment no matter where you went.

She had seen how tired Frank Kilburn was when he came in for supper. She had wondered, then, if they were going to grow old separately, he doing his work, she doing hers, with nothing more in the way of companionship than an occasional dance at the Odd Fellow's Hall.

She didn't want it that way. She wanted to be married, and she wanted to have a family. In her was an urge as old as time itself: to bear children, to hold them in her arms, to thus fulfill herself.

The trouble was Frank wouldn't speak. And according to custom, it was the man who had to speak. A girl couldn't just walk up to a man and ask him to marry her. Nothing would make a man run away faster than that.

There were other ways, of course; ancient ways that had been used by her friends with great success. Four of her school friends had gotten married before they were seventeen. All four had been pregnant at the time of their marriages, and all four marriages had been happy ones.

Yet trapping a man by becoming pregnant had always seemed dishonest to Jennie, and she had refused to use that trick. Now, she told herself bitterly, she was still single because of her silly honesty and all her friends were married and had families.

The breeze seemed cooler in the bed of the creek. The leaves stirred softly overhead, making a pleasant, rustling sound. Kilburn sat down on a fallen log. Jennie sat at his side but not too close. She was tempted to sit close, tempted to try and stir him up, but she did not. That damned honesty again, she told herself angrily. Making conversation, she asked, "What's going to happen to Glen?" and immediately realized she had asked him the same question earlier. As if he had forgotten, too, he said, "He'll probably be hanged. Or go to prison for a long, long time."

"Poor Glen."

He sat there, silent, not answering. His shoulders were slumped, and she wondered if his eyes were closed. Suddenly, with complete unexpectedness, anger surged through her. It made her face burn, made perspiration spring out all over her. She said in a choked up voice, "Damn you, Frank Kilburn! Oh damn you anyway!"

He straightened, silent for a moment, but finally asking, "What in God's name was that all about?"

"I'll tell you what it was about! I . . . You . . ." Suddenly she choked up so that she couldn't go on. She felt the hot flood of tears coming to her eyes. And then she was weeping, hysterically, without restraint or control.

For several moments she wept alone. Then she felt Frank draw her to her feet, felt his arms go around her awkwardly.

Her weeping continued, as if there were a flood inside her that had to be released. Frank's arms tightened, drawing her closer to him.

It began slowly, a fire deep within her, and it found an answering fire in Frank. He tilted her head back and with a callused hand wiped away her tears. His lips found hers, lightly at first, but with a demanding passion that increased and would not be denied.

Not that she wanted to deny it. Her own lips were as hungry, as eager as his. The fires mounted in her. She felt herself lifted and carried and laid in a bed of long, dry grass.

She wanted to cry out and refuse, tell him to stop, but no words came to her lips. There was only this fire in her that she had never felt before, mounting like a holocaust, devouring everything but the hunger to have him go on, to have him finish what he had began.

It ended like a burst of pyrotechnics on

the Fourth of July and left her weak, spent beside him on the ground.

For what seemed like a long time, they lay there side by side, still clinging to each other even though the pressing need was gone. Slowly Jennie began to realize that, despite her honesty, despite her determination not to trap him this way, she had done exactly that. Unless . . . unless she let him know right now that what had happened was in no way binding on him — to marry her or anything.

She pushed him away and struggled to her feet, hastily straightening her clothes, as angry now as she had been earlier. She said, "Don't worry. Nobody's going to ask anything of you just because of this."

Kilburn got to his feet. He said, with a touch of anger in his voice, "What is that supposed to mean?"

"It means you don't have to feel you've got to marry me just because of this." She was trembling and her voice quavered.

Frank said, "Jennie, for God's sake . . ."

"Don't you curse at me!" She was suddenly weeping again and unable to go on. He reached for her, but she eluded him and turned and ran.

He pursued her through the darkness but gave up the chase half a block from her house. He didn't want to chase her inside, panting and out of breath, her hair and clothing disarrayed. Her mother would know instantly what had happened to her.

He stopped and stared into the darkness in the direction she had gone, a puzzled frown on his face. Any man who claimed to understand women was a fool, he thought.

But he was more deeply moved than ever before in his life. Down there beside the creek Jennie had been all that any man could ever want.

Maybe she *would* marry him, he thought. Maybe now . . . He turned and headed back toward the center of town, thinking for the first time in his life what it would be like to have a home of his own, to have Jennie, to have kids to welcome him when he came home. But his frown remained because he wasn't too sure Jennie would ever speak to him again.

V

Kilburn walked slowly going back, cooling off, taking a roundabout route that brought him into Main at the upper end near the courthouse and the Methodist Church. All he could think about was Jennie. He wished

51

she had not been so angry when she left. Most of all, he hoped that overnight her anger would not harden into something too implacable to be overcome tomorrow.

Passing Judge Barngrover's house, he heard a voice call out from the judge's vine-covered porch. "Is that you, Frank?"

He turned in at the gate and approached the porch. "Good evening, Judge."

"I saw you bring Glen Epperson into town. Did you have any trouble taking him?"

"No sir. He didn't put up any fight. Glen's pretty decent, and he's never been in trouble with the law before."

"He killed a man. By shooting him in the back."

"Yes sir. I suppose he did."

"You're not excusing him?"

"No. But he's like a lot of other people hereabouts. He was pushed to the limit. If this heat and drought don't let up, there may be others doing what Glen did, or worse."

"That's what I want to talk to you about. We've got to do something to keep that from happening."

"Do something? What do you have in mind?"

"I want Glen Epperson brought to trial

immediately. I want him convicted, and I intend to sentence him to hang. I want to make an example of him so that if others are tempted to violence they may have some second thoughts."

Kilburn said, "You're the judge. I guess that's up to you."

"You don't approve?"

Kilburn hesitated. It wasn't his place to criticize the judge. But neither did he believe that Glen Epperson should be used as an example for anyone. Glen was entitled to be tried strictly on the merits of his own case with no other considerations influencing his trial. He said, "No, if I'm going to be honest with you, I've got to say I don't."

"Why not?" Kilburn could hear the porch swing squeak as the judge swung back and forth. It was a little cooler here but not very much.

He said, "Well, I think a man is entitled to be tried for whatever crime he actually committed. I don't think he ought to be used as an example for anyone."

"Are you trying to say he won't get a fair trial in my court?"

"I'm not *trying* to say anything." Irritation was stirring in Kilburn, however hard he tried to quiet it. "You asked me if I disapproved and I answered you."

"I don't think I like your implication." The judge's voice was stern, the way Kilburn had sometimes heard it sound in court.

Kilburn said, "A man's supposed to be presumed innocent until he's proven guilty. But you just said you wanted him convicted and that you intended to sentence him to hang. And he hasn't even been brought to trial."

"There are a dozen witnesses . . ."

"Yes, sir. But a man's still entitled to his day in court — in a fair and impartial court."

There was a long silence. Kilburn half expected Judge Barngrover to explode, but he did not. He cleared his throat and said, with a certain humility in his voice, "I'm sorry, Frank. I guess you're right. But I still want Epperson brought to trial immediately. It may keep something else from happening. I'll see John Gardell first thing in the morning. And I'll ask Ed Burke to defend Epperson."

Gardell was the county attorney and it would be his job to prosecute. Ed Burke was the only other lawyer in town, and unless Epperson insisted on someone from another town, he would have to be defended by Ed Burke.

Kilburn asked, "Was that all you wanted

to see me about?"

"Yes, Frank. That was all." The porch swung squeaked thunderously as the judge stood up. "Good night."

"Good night, Judge." Kilburn went down the walk to the gate. He heard the judge's screen door slam.

Wearily he walked toward the center of town. The only lights still visible were at the saloon and in the lobby of the hotel. It had been a long day, he thought. It had been a long two days. He hadn't slept at all last night worrying about Epperson.

He started into the hotel but stopped when he heard loud voices from the direction of the saloon. He thought, "Oh Lord, not something else!" and walked swiftly toward the sounds.

The voices were shouting now, but he still couldn't recognize any of them. He reached the saloon and stepped in through the open door.

Ross Lockhart was doing most of the yelling, and it was obvious that he was drunk. Ute Willis stood across the bar from him, his face red, beads of sweat standing out on his forehead. He interrupted Lockhart and bawled, "No! I said no, damn it! No! No more credit until you pay somethin' on what you owe!"

"You dirty old sonofabitch! I been tradin' here for years, an' I always paid you cash until this year! If there was another saloon in town you could just go straight to hell!"

"Don't call me no sonofabitch. Just get out of here before I throw you out."

Standing in the doorway, Kilburn pulled out his watch and looked at it. It was a little past ten o'clock.

He started across the room toward Lockhart. He hated to throw Lockhart in jail, but he couldn't see any help for it. Lockhart's hired man, Tako Nomura, was standing at the end of the bar, shaking, looking scared.

Suddenly, Ute Willis reached underneath the bar. Kilburn knew instantly what he was reaching for, and so, apparently, did Lockhart. Kilburn opened his mouth to yell at Ute, but the words never came out. Lockhart leaped onto the bar and from there jumped on Ute Willis like a mountain lion.

It surprised Kilburn. He had thought Lockhart too drunk to put up much of a fight. Ute disappeared behind the bar, and Lockhart also disappeared. Kilburn roared, "Stop it, both of you! Stop it or I'll throw you both in jail!"

From behind the bar, the shotgun roared. The charge shattered the back bar mirror and at least a dozen bottles of whiskey sitting in front of it. Kilburn was running now. He raced past Nomura, who was cowering like a frightened mouse. He rounded the end of the bar, fully prepared to see one or both men bleeding from the shotgun charge.

But neither man seemed to have been hurt. They were wrestling for possession of the gun, which still had a charge left in the other barrel. Kilburn roared again, "Stop it! Before I bust some heads!"

Neither Lockhart nor Willis seemed to hear. Or perhaps, he thought, both were afraid to let go of the gun. Kilburn drew his revolver and stepped close to the two struggling on the floor. The place reeked of whiskey, which had drenched both combatants. Broken glass littered the floor, but so far neither man appeared to have been cut.

Kilburn jammed his revolver muzzle into Lockhart's ear. "Let go or I'll blow a hole in you!"

Lockhart turned his head and glanced up at Frank. He released the gun. Ute Willis, red with fury, struggled to his knees. Holding the gun in both hands, he brought it savagely around so that the butt struck Lockhart above the ear. Lockhart slumped and sprawled out unconscious on the floor.

Ute Willis made it to his feet. Kilburn said

furiously, "You didn't have to do that! If he's hurt . . ."

Willis said harshly, "He ain't hurt. That bastard's got solid marble for a head."

Kilburn slammed his gun back into its holster and turned his head to look at Nomura. "Go get Doc Peabody. Tell him to come to the jail."

Turning back, Kilburn spoke angrily to Ute. "Help me carry him to the jail."

"Hell, I can't leave here."

Kilburn said with cold anger, "Either you help me carry him to the jail or spend the night there yourself. Make up your mind and do it fast!"

"All right. All right. No need to get so feisty about it."

Kilburn lifted Lockhart's head and shoulders. Willis lifted his feet. The two carried the unconscious man out of the saloon and across the street to the jail. They laid him down while Kilburn unlocked the door. He had left a lamp burning inside. Epperson was still asleep.

There was only one cell, but there were two cots in it. Kilburn unlocked the cell door and went back out to help Willis carry Lockhart in. Lockhart left a trail of blood from a glass cut on his right forearm.

Once he had been laid on the couch, Kilburn looked at Willis. "Get out of here."

Willis scowled but meekly went outside. Kilburn brought the lamp into the cell and looked at Lockhart's forearm. The cut was deep but the bleeding was steady, so he knew the glass hadn't cut an artery.

Epperson woke up. "What's going on?"

Kilburn said, "You got company."

"Who is it?"

"Ross Lockhart."

"What'd *he* do?"

"Got in a fight with Ute."

Epperson sat up on his bunk. Kilburn went out to the street door, carrying the lamp. He was worried about Lockhart. Ute had hit the man pretty hard. He looked up the street in the direction from which he knew Doc Peabody would come, but the street was empty and dark.

He put down the lamp. Irritably he began to pace back and forth. He was tired and he wanted to go to bed, but there could be no sleep for him until Doc had examined Lockhart and treated him. Even then he wouldn't dare sleep in his own room at the hotel. He'd have to spend the night here at the jail.

Epperson's cot creaked as he got up. Kilburn said, "Stay right where you are. I don't want any trouble with you."

"All I want is a drink of water."

"Stay put. I'll bring it to you." He got a dipper of water from the bucket on the washstand in the corner of the office and carried it back to Glen. Glen drank it thirstily and handed the dipper back. By the time Kilburn had hung it beside the bucket, Doc Peabody was at the door. "Tako says Lockhart is hurt."

He was an oldish man, whom Kilburn judged to be about sixty-five. He had a white complexion and very few whiskers, which made him look a little womanish. The impression was heightened by his wide hips and small delicate hands. But he was a good doctor, skillful and methodical. He could treat a gunshot wound, deliver a baby, or treat an ailing horse with equal professionalism. Kilburn said, "Uh huh. Ute Willis knocked him out. He's got a bad cut on his left forearm, and he might have others, too. He and Ute were fighting behind the bar, and some bottles got broken."

Doc Peabody carried his bag back into the cell. "I'll need more light. Have you got another lamp?"

Kilburn lighted a second lamp and carried it back into the cell. He put it on a shelf over Lockhart's cot. Doc was already examining the man.

Kilburn went back to the office and sat down. He lighted his pipe. His eyes were heavy and he had trouble keeping them open. He wished Doc would hurry.

He said, "If you don't mind, Doc, I'll lock you in. I want to go over and close the saloon."

"I don't mind."

Kilburn locked the cell door and went out into the street. He crossed to the saloon. There were eight men in the place, some ranchers, some men from the town. He said, "Close up, Ute."

"What for?"

"Because I just told you to."

"You can't come in here and tell me to close. Who the hell do you think you are?"

Kilburn looked steadily at him. "Want to push it?"

Ute Willis met his glance for several moments, but in the end he looked away. His face darker, he called, "All right, boys, it's time to close. Finish your drinks and go on home."

Kilburn waited, standing to one side so that the men could leave. When the last one had gone, Willis came to the door. Kilburn stepped outside, and Ute slammed the door angrily and locked it.

Kilburn crossed the street to the jail. Doc

was bandaging Lockhart's arm. Lockhart was stirring, and Kilburn asked, "That knock on his head — is it serious?"

"Concussion. He may vomit some of that rotgut he drank, and he'll have the king of all headaches when he wakes up. But I think he'll be all right. I'll look in on him tomorrow."

Kilburn let him out of the cell, locked it, then followed him to the door. Doc said, "If this heat doesn't let up, there'll be more broken heads than his."

Kilburn said, "Good night, Doc. And thanks."

Peabody walked away, a little stooped, his black bag in his hand. Kilburn closed and locked the door. He told Epperson to blow out the lamp in the cell but he left the one in the office burning, turning it very low.

He lay down on the couch without even taking off his boots and closed his eyes. He was instantly asleep.

VI

Kilburn was awakened at dawn by a thunderous knocking on the door. He sat up groggily, immediately recognizing the fact that he was in the jail instead of his room at the hotel. He got to his feet and stumbled across the room. He unbolted the door and opened it.

Oscar Tafoya was there, accompanied by two of his sons. Instantly, Kilburn knew something was wrong. Tafoya's wagon was drawn up in the street outside the jail. The sheepman's face was pale. His two sons seemed numb, as though something had happened to them that they couldn't understand. Kilburn asked, "What is it, Oscar?"

Tafoya cleared his throat. He swallowed twice before he could speak and when he did, his voice was hoarse and choked. "Domingo's dead."

"Dead? How? What happened?"

Tafoya gestured toward the wagon with his head. His mouth was working and his eyes were glazed. Kilburn stepped out onto the walk and crossed to the wagon.

The supplies for which Tafoya and his sons had come to town yesterday were still in the wagon. But in a cleared area lay the body of Domingo, Tafoya's youngest son.

The rising sun put a glare of light on the body, showing every abrasion, every bit of dirt and dust, every rent and tear in the dusty clothes. Domingo's eyes were closed, his face very pale in death. There was a caved-in place at one side of his head as big as the palm of Kilburn's hand. Blood had run from it and dried. Now it was almost black. A green-bodied fly settled on the wound, and Kilburn shooed the fly away.

He knew instantly how Domingo had died. He had been dragged at the end of a rope. Bits of sagebrush still adhered to his dusty clothes. The abrasions, scabbed with a mixture of dust and blood, were unmistakable. So were the rope burns on his upper arms and chest and back, where his shirt had been torn while he was being dragged. Kilburn looked at Oscar Tafoya and his lips formed one unnecessary word, "Who?"

Tafoya shook his head. "It was dark — too dark to follow trail, and I didn't want to spoil what tracks there were by stumbling around by lantern light. But we both know who. Hugo Enzbarger has been talking against sheep and Mexicans all summer long. Eight dead sheep were lying in the road. I figure Hugo's sons tried to ride through the sheep and when they couldn't, started shooting them. Domingo interfered and was roped and dragged."

Kilburn shook his head helplessly. "Oscar, I can't tell you how sorry I am." The words seemed stupid and inadequate.

Tafoya raised his head. He looked Kilburn in the eye. "Sorry ain't enough. I want you to find the one that dragged Domingo to death. I want you to bring him in, and I want to watch him hang."

"I'll bring him in."

"You'd better. Because if the law don't do the job, us Tafoyas will."

Kilburn nodded mutely. He put a hand on Tafoya's shoulder and gripped it sympathetically. This expression of compassion was suddenly too much for Tafoya. He doubled over the side of the wagon and buried his face in his hands. His shoulders shook.

Kilburn looked at the faces of Tafoya's sons. They were shocked and pale and embarrassed to see their father weeping thus. Kilburn said, "Take Domingo down to Littlejohn's."

Jasper Littlejohn had a furniture store next to his mercantile store. In the rear was an undertaking parlor, where a selection of coffins lined one wall. Kilburn said, "I'll go tell Mr. Littlejohn and ask him to come down."

Tafoya's two sons nodded, still looking at their father with that shocked pain in their eyes. Kilburn turned and locked the door of the jail. Inside, Lockhart was yelling, but he didn't take time to find out why.

Swiftly he walked uptown to Jasper Littlejohn's house. Littlejohn's youngest son,

Tommy, was pouring a bucket of water on some of his mother's flowers growing beside the porch. Kilburn asked, "Your pa still here?"

"Yes sir. He's inside. Want me to tell him you're here?"

"Uh huh. Tell him it's important."

Tommy ran into the house, a thin, serious boy about ten years old. After several moments, Jasper Littlejohn came to the door. He stepped out onto the porch immediately, a napkin still in his hand. "I'm eating breakfast, Frank. Will you come in and have a bite?"

Kilburn shook his head. "Oscar Tafoya's son, Domingo, has been killed. Oscar's down at your place with the body now. I wonder if you'd mind going down."

"Of course not." Littlejohn turned and hurried into the house, a tall, strongly built man of sixty, who still put in ten hours every day at his store. Kilburn guessed he had been pretty well-to-do until this year. Maybe he still was. But he'd given a lot of credit to the ranchers on Red Creek, and there was no assurance that he would ever collect from them.

Littlejohn came out, hat on, shrugging into his coat. He walked swiftly toward the center of town and for half a block Kilburn kept pace. "How did it happen?" Littlejohn asked.

"He was dragged. Oscar said there were eight dead sheep lying in the road."

"Enzbarger?"

"Hugo was in town last night. He left just a little while before the Tafoyas did so I doubt if it was him. It would have been too late by the time he went by the Tafoya place."

Littlejohn nodded. If he thought Domingo had been killed by Enzbarger's sons, he didn't say so. In front of Mrs. Reagan's boardinghouse, Kilburn left the storekeeper and went up to the door. He stepped inside, to find the boarders at the long table eating breakfast.

Dan Massey glanced up at him. Kilburn said, "Can I see you a minute, Dan?"

Massey was a young man, as brawny as a blacksmith. He had a friendly, cheerful grin. He nodded and came into the parlor where Kilburn stood. Kilburn said, "Domingo Tafoya has been killed, and I've got to ride up there and read some sign. Do you want to look after the jail for me?"

"Sure. Have I got time to finish breakfast?"

"Uh huh. But come as soon as you've finished."

Massey went back to the table. It was typical of him that he hadn't asked a lot of questions, and Kilburn knew he wouldn't tell anybody that Domingo had been killed.

He walked slowly back toward the jail, frowning. He didn't like the idea of going to the Enzbarger place all by himself. Hugo Enzbarger's sons were a wild, unruly bunch, and there was no telling what they might do. On the other hand, he didn't want to form a posse, at least until he was sure there was a need for it. The way tempers were in Guthrie and on Red Creek, he doubted if he could control the possemen, and, besides, he wanted to be free to read what sign there was without interference from anyone.

A block from the intersection of Main and First, he glanced behind. Tommy Littlejohn was just turning into the alley half a block east of First, on his way to his father's store. Kilburn grinned faintly to himself because it was so typical of a ten year old to prefer an alley to a street.

When he reached Main, he heard a shrill yell behind him and turned. Tommy Littlejohn had just run out of the alley behind the bank. He shrilled, "Sheriff! Sheriff Kilburn!"

Kilburn walked toward him. Out of breath, Tommy panted, "The back door of the bank is open, Sheriff! I think somebody might be robbin' it."

Kilburn broke into a run. As he passed Tommy, he said, "Go on down to your father's store," knowing the instant he said it that Tommy would not obey. Running, he turned into the alley behind the bank.

He had gone to sleep last night wearing boots and clothes and even his holstered gun and belt, so the gun was still in its holster at his side. He dragged it out and ran into the back door of the bank, his thumb on the hammer ready to draw it back.

No one was in the bank, but then he hadn't really expected there would be anyone. The minute Tommy had said the back door of the bank was open, he had thought of Lockhart, whom he had caught in the alley about eight o'clock the night before. Lockhart must have gotten in, he thought.

He turned in time to see Nelson Struthers step into the back door. Struthers asked, "Anybody here?"

Kilburn shook his head. "Take a look around. See what he took."

Struthers hurried toward the front part of the bank.

Kilburn went to the alley entrance and

looked at the door. It had been pried open with a bar, the main lock and an auxiliary hasp and padlock broken. The bar lay in the alley beside the door. It had to have been Lockhart, he thought. But if it had, where had Lockhart cached the loot?

Hearing footsteps, he turned. Struthers was approaching him, a worried look upon his face. Kilburn asked, "What did he take?"

Struthers shook his head. "Nothing."

"What do you mean, nothing? A man don't break into a bank for fun. He must have taken something."

Struthers shook his head again. "Nothing is gone."

"Then what are you looking so damned worried about? I'd think you'd be relieved."

"I *am* relieved. Of course, I'm relieved."

Frowning, Kilburn stared at him. Struthers looked away. Kilburn asked, "Is anything misplaced?"

Struthers shook his head, looking at the floor. Kilburn knew he was lying, but he couldn't understand why Struthers would lie to him.

Struthers was a short, paunchy, graying man in a gray business suit. His face was red and bathed with sweat, and he was trembling, Kilburn said, "All right. I guess what I don't need right now is a bank robbery." He went out the back door and down the alley. He saw Jennie Morgan peering out the window of the restaurant, and that reminded him that sometime today he had to find time to talk to her, to straighten out what had happened last night if it was possible.

He hurried along the street to the livery barn. The wind had already begun to blow, and the barn was creaking threateningly. Kilburn glanced up at it. It looked solid enough, but it sure made a racket in the wind.

He went inside. He owned two horses, which was a good thing because he had certainly worn out the one he'd ridden after Epperson. He saddled the other one, a big gray, mounted and rode out into the street. He rode to the jail, dismounted and tied.

Dan Massey was already there. Kilburn said, "Go on up to the restaurant and get three meals. I'll wait until you get back."

He unlocked the jail door then went back and unlocked the cell. Lockhart was scowling, and whenever he moved his head, he winced. He must have a monstrous headache, Kilburn thought. He said, "Somebody broke into the bank last night."

Lockhart didn't answer that immediately.

When he did, it was to ask, "How much did he get?"

"That's the funny part. He didn't take anything. It's a good thing, too, because if anything was missing, I'd have to arrest you, bein' as I caught you in the alley behind the bank last night."

"I told you why I was there."

"Sure. Sure you did. What were you lookin' for, anyway?"

Lockhart lowered his glance and stared at the floor. Kilburn said, "Maybe I ought to hold you, just in case. Struthers might find something missing after he's had time to look around."

"He won't . . . I mean, I thought you said nothing was done."

"I did. But . . ."

"You can't hold me! All I did was to get slugged in the head." Lockhart stared at Kilburn worriedly, and Kilburn wondered why be was so worried about the possibility of spending the day in jail.

He said, "You act like you were afraid Struthers *might* find something gone."

"He won't find nothing gone."

"Because you didn't take anything?"

"That ain't what I said." Lockhart's tone became pleading. "Don't keep me here all

72

day. I'm sick. I want to go home and go to bed."

Kilburn shrugged. "All right. Go on. But get out of town. I've had enough trouble with you to last me awhile."

Lockhart's face was vastly relieved. He got his hat and hurried out. Kilburn looked at Epperson. "Want to go to the outhouse and then get washed up?"

Epperson nodded, and Kilburn followed him out the door. He was sure that Lockhart had broken into the bank. He was equally sure that Lockhart had already left it when he caught him in the alley last night.

Which meant Lockhart hadn't meant to rob the place when he broke in. And if he hadn't, then he must have been looking for something else.

Information, perhaps. Maybe the name of whoever owned the mortgages on all the ranches along Red Creek.

He must have gotten the information, Kilburn thought. And if he had, it would explain his eagerness to get out of jail. It would also explain Struthers's obvious worry, even though he'd said nothing was missing from the bank.

He saw Nelson Struthers cross the street to the livery barn as he brought Epperson back into the front door of the jail. Struthers came out several minutes later, driving a buggy. He turned the corner and took the Red Creek road.

Dan Massey brought the three meals. He took one into the cell to Epperson. Kilburn sat down and ate a second one. The third, Lockhart's, would have to go to waste.

When he had finished, Kilburn grabbed a shotgun and a handful of shells, nodded at Massey, then went out and mounted his horse. He took the Red Creek road. When he got out of town and on a straightaway, he could see the dust of Struthers's buggy about a mile ahead.

VII

Nelson Struthers turned in at the lane that led to Adam Guthrie's place. As Kilburn rode past the gate, he could see the buggy standing in the shade of the giant poplars that surrounded Guthrie's house. He couldn't see Struthers, so he supposed the banker had gone inside.

Struthers's action in coming here so precipitously told Kilburn a lot of things. It told him that Lockhart had indeed broken into the bank last night looking for information. It told him Lockhart had found what he was looking for, else Struthers would not have been so concerned. It also told him that Guthrie was the one who had bought up all the mortgages on Red Creek. And knowing that, a lot of other things suddenly became very clear.

Guthrie must not want the loans repaid. He must want them to default, and in this the weather was playing right into his hands. Guthrie probably envisioned himself owning one gigantic ranch reaching all the way from the town of Guthrie to the head of Red Creek forty miles away.

Furthermore, if he owned all the land along Red Creek, he would control the plateau on both sides of it, giving him an abundance of summer range. He would have one of the biggest and best ranches in the entire state.

But Guthrie's ambitions weren't Kilburn's prime concern today. He withdrew the double-barreled shotgun he had brought in place of his rifle from the saddle boot and broke the action. He took two shells loaded with buckshot out of his pocket and placed them in the gun. He closed the action with a snap, then shoved the gun back into the boot.

He kept his horse at a steady trot, an easy gait for the animal to maintain over a long period of time. He was fully aware of the chance he took. The Enzbargers were tough and hard. If one of them had killed Domingo Tafoya, they'd stand together in that one's defense, against the law, against the Tafoyas, against whoever came after them.

But he also was aware that if he took a posse up Red Creek to the Enzbargers' place, the Enzbargers would probably all be killed. So would some of the possemen.

Yet how he could capture the guilty one, all by himself, he had no clear idea. He supposed he would have to work out some plan when he found out what he was up against.

The morning hours dragged. One by one, he passed the burned out ranches along Red Creek. In the yards of some he glimpsed a man or woman working, but no one was in the barren hay fields, and most of the places seemed deserted.

Along the creek, when the road dipped near to it, he saw gaunt, half-starved cattle standing listlessly in whatever shade was available. And as he rode, the heat steadily increased.

Twice, he watered his horse in the creek. Once he got down and drank of the brackish, alkali water himself, afterward splashing it into his face and over his head. It was mid-afternoon before he glimpsed the Tafoya wagon in the distance.

The untended sheep were spread out near the creek. A bell tinkled here and there. Buzzards circled over the place where the dead sheep lay.

Short of the nearest one, Kilburn dismounted and tied his horse to a clump of brush. Eyes squinted against the glare, he approached on foot. Without seeming to, he scanned the hillsides nearest him, but he didn't see anything.

The road was pitted with the tracks of sheep overlying which the tracks of the Tafoya wagon were visible. Beyond the carcasses, which were bloated and covered with flies, he came upon the tracks of several horses and a little farther on, on the mark of a body in the dust. This place was surrounded by boot tracks, and here the tracks of the Tafoya wagon showed that the wagon had been turned around. Going on, Kilburn left the road and traced the trail left by Domingo's body up the gully east of it.

It wasn't hard to find the tracks of the horse whose rider had dragged Domingo to death. Kilburn knelt and studied them, frowning as he did. By now he was sure that he was being watched. He could feel it.

There was a bad split in the horse's right rear hoof. Kilburn straightened. The horse would be easy to trail, easy to identify when he was found. He walked back to the road, studied the ground above the bodies of the dead sheep for a few moments more, then went back and untied his horse. Mounting, he continued up the road, riding at a steady walk.

If they shot him, he doubted if he'd ever hear the report. The bullet would come as a blow in the middle of his back, driving him forward out of the saddle. Perhaps there would be a brief period of awareness, perhaps none. But he didn't dare look around. He didn't dare let on that he was aware of being watched. That in itself might be enough to bring a bullet from the unseen watcher's gun.

There were a lot of horse tracks in the road, some of them fresh, some not. He picked out those of three horses besides the one with the split rear hoof. The tracks of Hugo Enzbarger's horse were easily identifiable because they overlaid the tracks of the other three.

Half an hour later, Kilburn found the Enzbarger place in sight. It sat right next to the creek and was surrounded by cottonwoods. Kilburn didn't glance up at it. He kept studying the tracks in the road as though oblivious of everything else.

The gate stood open. The hayfields were almost as barren as the road. A few scrawny cattle stood in the shade of the cottonwoods. Kilburn rode slowly down the lane.

Entering the yard, he did not dismount but followed the split hoofprint straight to the corral. The sensation of being watched was stronger now, because he was being watched from the house as well as from the brush.

Three horses were in the circular pole corral. He dismounted, opened the gate and went inside. The horses spooked away from him.

He took down a rope that was hanging on the corral, and shook out a loop. He caught the horses one by one and examined their right rear hooves. He hadn't expected to find the split hoof and he did not. But he had proved, to his own satisfaction at least, that Domingo had been killed by one of Enzbarger's sons. Before he was through he would know which one.

Cautiously and furtively, he scanned the surrounding area as he paused beside his horse to pack and fill his pipe. He let his glance rest briefly on the house.

It was built of hand-hewn logs and chinked with adobe mud. It was not a large house. He had never been inside, but it

79

didn't look as though it contained more than three small rooms. On the south side there was a lean-to. In front there were two windows, over which blinds were drawn, and a door. The ground in front of the door was white with an accumulation of soap from the dishwater emptied off the stoop.

Kilburn lighted his pipe and puffed comfortably for several moments. He fully expected the door to open, but it did not. He picked up his horse's reins and, still puffing, swung to the horse's back. He rode toward the house at a leisurely walk.

Just short of it, he suddenly dug spurs into his horse's sides. He guided the horse toward the lean-to and, snatching the shotgun out of the saddle boot, hit the ground running. He reached the side of the lean-to and skidded to a halt, nervously hoping the unseen watcher didn't, even now, have him in his rifle's sights.

He cocked one of the shotgun's hammers and poked the gun muzzle around the corner. He heard the door bolt shoot back and saw the door open. Hugo Enzbarger stepped outside, a rifle in his hands.

Kilburn said, "Drop it, Hugo! At this range I can cut you in two."

Hugo Enzbarger stared into the gaping bores of the double-barreled ten gauge. Kilburn added harshly, "It's loaded with buck."

Hugo dropped the rifle. Kilburn said, "Now tell your boys to drop their guns and come outside."

Hugo met his glance defiantly. "They've got 'em lined on you right now. I'd say it was a Mexican standoff. I'd say you'll be damn lucky to get out of this alive."

Kilburn called, "Come on out, boys, but drop your guns before you do."

One of the boys' voices said, "You drop yours, Sheriff. I've got my gun lined on your belly, and you've got just half a minute before I shoot."

Kilburn didn't move. Softly he said, "I'd talk to those boys of yours if I was you, Hugo. They might get me, like they say, but even if they do, this shotgun is going off. Could be it'll miss you, but I sure don't think it will."

For a long moment, Hugo Enzbarger studied Kilburn's face. At last he growled, "Do what he says, boys. That shotgun's lined on my belly, and he'll get the trigger pulled even if you kill him with your first shot."

Again there was a long silence. Kilburn felt his knees trembling and he hoped Enzbarger couldn't see. There was an angry curse from inside the house and the door opened. Rudy and Sam came out, their hands empty.

Kilburn said, "Line up facing the house. Put both hands over your heads."

Sullenly they obeyed. Kilburn approached Hugo first. He put the shotgun muzzle against the base of Hugo's skull, holding it with just one hand. With the other, he slapped Hugo's pockets. He found a sheathed hunting knife in the right side pocket of Hugo's pants.

He tossed it away, then moved on to Sam, the second one. He knew that Karl was somewhere behind him, probably with a rifle, so he was careful to keep the shotgun pointed at one of the Enzbargers all the time. He found nothing on Sam, but he found a large clasp knife on Rudy.

He thought, it must be a hundred and ten degrees in this sunbaked yard. He could feel sweat running down his sides and back. Stepping away, he wiped a sleeve across his forehead to keep the sweat from running down into his eyes. He asked, "Which of your boys dragged Tafoya's son, Hugo?"

"None of 'em." Hugo's voice was a surly growl. He kept turning his head and looking beyond Kilburn, as if expecting Karl to suddenly appear. His face changed slightly, and Kilburn stepped forward and put the shotgun muzzle against his head once more. "Tell him to come in."

"You go to hell!"

Kilburn put a patience into his voice that he didn't feel. "Hugo, I'm either going to take in one of you, or I'm going to take you all. Now you make up your goddamn mind and do it fast. I'm hot and tired, and I'm as edgy as everybody else in this country is."

Sam interrupted, "Don't tell him, Pa."

Kilburn said, "And tell Karl to come on in. Tell him to come unarmed if he don't want to see his pa's head blown off."

Hugo growled, "You wouldn't shoot."

"Wouldn't I? Think about that, Hugo. I can kill you with one barrel, and I've still got a chance to get your two boys with the other before they can get me. That just leaves Karl."

"We'll let you go back to town. You back off and I give you my word we'll let you go."

Kilburn repeated, "Tell Karl to come in." Suddenly impatient, he rammed the shotgun muzzle harder against Hugo's head. "Do it! Now!"

Hugo's face lost a bit of color as his glance found Kilburn's angry stare. He called, "Karl! Drop your gun and come on in!"

Kilburn heard footsteps shuffling across

the yard. Karl came into his field of vision, and he said, "Up against the house, beside your brothers. Hands on the wall above your head."

Karl obeyed, looking scared. Kilburn stepped back, now covering all of them. "Empty your pockets, Karl. Turn them inside out."

Karl obeyed. One side pocket held a fist-sized rock. Kilburn said, "All right, head for the corral. Two of you can ride double. Unless you want to tell me who dragged Domingo to death."

Karl said, "Pa, you ain't goin' to tell him, are you?"

"You got a better idea? He's either goin' to take the one who dragged Domingo or he's goin' to take us all. And whos' goin' to help us if we're all in jail?"

None of Hugo's three sons answered. Kilburn said, "Well?"

"It was Rudy. You go ahead and take him. But don't count on keepin' him."

Kilburn said, "All right, Rudy. Saddle up a horse." He picked up the reins of his own horse without letting the shotgun muzzle stray. He swung the gun to point at Rudy's back and followed him across the yard to the corral.

Rudy went in and roped himself a horse.

He took a weathered saddle off the top corral pole, threw it on and cinched it down. Kilburn mounted and rode up close. He said, "Don't get any ideas about tryin' to get away. This thing has a range of fifty yards, and it's impossible to miss with it."

Rudy only scowled. He mounted and rode slowly up the dusty lane toward the road. Kilburn followed less than half dozen feet behind.

He didn't bother to look back. He didn't know whether they'd try to follow him or not. What he did know was that the shotgun was going to be pointed straight at Rudy all the way to town. It was the only way he could be sure he'd stay alive.

VIII

Kilburn stayed a few paces behind Rudy Enzbarger all afternoon. At dusk, fearing Rudy might try escaping in the dark, he dropped the loop of his rope over Rudy's head, pulled it tight, and secured the end to his saddle horn. He kept the shotgun pointed at his prisoner, but the rope made it less likely that he would have to shoot.

It was well after dark when the two rode into town. Kilburn headed straight for the jail. He dismounted wearily and watched as Rudy followed suit, the rope still around his waist. Without removing it, Kilburn gestured toward the door. Rudy went inside.

Dan Massey was sitting at the desk. Kilburn said, "Put him in with Epperson."

Dan went back and unlocked the cell. He took the rope off Rudy and stood aside while he went into the cell. He closed and locked the door.

Kilburn slumped into a chair. The thought occurred to him that in all the five years he'd been sheriff, nobody had been accused of anything more serious than butchering someone else's steer. Now he had two men, both accused of murder. He wondered where it was going to end.

Dan was staring at him, an odd expression on his face. "Have any trouble taking him?"

Kilburn shook his head.

"Hugo and the other two brothers gave him up? Just like that?"

Kilburn grinned. "I had this shotgun. They decided not to argue with it."

Dan said, "Go get yourself a drink. I can go up to the restaurant and get Rudy his supper."

Kilburn shook his head. "You stay here." He handed the shotgun to Dan. "Keep this handy. His old man might try to break him out."

He got up wearily and went outside. He crossed to the saloon and ordered a beer. He drank it thirstily and ordered another one.

Ed Burke was standing at the end of the bar. He picked up his drink and came to where Kilburn stood. "You look just about worn out."

"I am. It's been hot."

"Get the man who killed Domingo Tafoya?"

Kilburn nodded.

"Who was it?"

"Rudy."

"Is he in jail?"

Kilburn nodded again. "What about the trial?"

"Epperson's? It's going to start day after tomorrow. Notices have already been delivered to the prospective jurors."

"You defending him?"

"Uh huh."

Kilburn studied him. Burke was a tall, thin young man in his late twenties. Kilburn said, "Try and get a postponement."

"Why?"

"Epperson will get a fairer trial in a month or two. Barngrover's going to try making an example out of him. He told me so."

"He won't give me a continuance."

"Try. Get the trial delayed until the weather has cooled off."

Burke shrugged. "I'll try. But it won't do any good."

Kilburn gulped his beer. He left two nickels on the bar and went outside. Ute Willis had studiously avoided looking at him, even when he drew and served his beer.

He walked up the street to the intersection and then crossed diagonally to the restaurant, relieved to see a light in it. He went inside, feeling dusty and dirty and knowing he probably smelled like a billy goat.

Tafoya and his two sons were in the restaurant. Jennie was behind the counter, wiping it with a rag. Her glance met his and dropped away.

Kilburn sat down at the counter. Jennie forced herself to look at him. He said, "I know it's late, but I haven't had anything to eat all day. Can you fix me something. And something for Rudy Enzbarger?"

She nodded without speaking and went to the kitchen. Oscar Tafoya came to the counter and sat beside him. His two sons sat down next to him. "Did I hear you say you had Rudy Enzbarger in jail?"

Kilburn nodded.

"Then he's the one?"

Kilburn said, "I trailed a horse with a split hoof to Enzbarger's place. I told Hugo I was going to jail them all unless they told me who dragged your boy. Hugo said it was Rudy. That's all I've got. Hugo is capable of telling me it was Rudy just so the one who really did it will have time to get away."

"You think Hugo is that sly?"

Kilburn hesitated. He didn't think Hugo was. He shook his head. "He didn't have time to think it out. I had a shotgun on him and his boys. I think Rudy was the one."

"Then he'll hang."

Kilburn stared at Tafoya's face. He looked beyond at the faces of his sons. They were angry and unyielding. He said, "I read all the sign up there. Rudy didn't mean to kill your son. He didn't drag him very far. Domingo's head just happened to hit a rock."

Tafoya scowled. "Don't make excuses for that murderer."

Kilburn said patiently, "I'm not making excuses. But don't expect him to go on trial for murder. Manslaughter, maybe, but not murder."

"He dragged Domingo. Just because we are Mexicans, you are going to let him get away with it."

Kilburn shook his head. "I brought him in. That's as far as my job goes. The rest is up to the court."

Tafoya was silent for a long time. His face was dark, his eyes angry. Behind him, his two sons glowered. At last the sheepman stood up. Warningly he said, "If Rudy Enzbarger does not hang . . . if he is released, then we will get justice in our own way, ourselves."

Kilburn was tired of being threatened. He was tired of being told how to do his job. He was worn out and hungry and hot, and his temper was rising dangerously. He said softly, "Don't threaten me, Mr. Tafoya. Unless you want to be in the same jail cell as Rudy Enzbarger and Glen Epperson."

Tafoya's oldest son, Joseph, said angrily, "No use arguin' with him, Pa. A Mexican can't get a fair deal in this town."

Kilburn didn't argue because he knew argument wasn't going to change anything. Jennie brought his meal and he began to eat, ignoring Tafoya and his sons. Tafoya got up sullenly, and all three left the restaurant, slamming the door furiously.

Kilburn looked at Jennie. Color had crept up into her face. He said, "I want to talk to you, but not tonight. I'm too wore out."

"I don't want to talk to you. We have nothing to say to each other. Nothing at all."

He felt a volatile rashness rising in him, and for an instant he understood how Glen Epperson had felt when he shot Miller Gross, how the Enzbarger brothers had felt when the sheep they hated so had blocked their way. He felt like doing something violent and rash himself. He clenched his jaws, holding back his reply. When he did speak, it was to say, "Thanks for getting supper for me. Is Rudy's supper ready?"

Without speaking, she turned and disappeared into the kitchen.

Maggie Morgan, busy washing dishes, glanced at her daughter's face. She had heard the exchange between Frank Kilburn and Jennie, and now she asked, "What was that all about?"

Jennie flushed. Maggie shrugged. "All right, so it's private. I didn't mean to pry." She returned her attention to her dishes.

She knew something had happened the night before. She thought she knew what it had been. And from her own experience, she understood how Jennie felt. Jennie's emotions had run away with her, and now she felt guilty and ashamed. She didn't want Frank Kilburn to get the idea she intended to use what had happened to trap him into a proposal. Only in trying to prove to him that he needn't ask her to marry him, she would probably drive him away.

She turned her head and opened her mouth to speak, then closed it again. This was neither the place nor the time.

Jennie was almost thirty. She wanted a husband and a family, and she was feeling a little desperate. Maggie understood that. She had been close to thirty herself when Jennie's father had finally asked her to marry him.

For five years now Jennie had wanted Frank Kilburn. Ever since he became sheriff here. And even though she had discouraged other men who might have courted her, Frank had accepted her with casual matter-of-factness, as if such a relationship could go on indefinitely.

Jennie carried the tray in to the front part of the restaurant. Maggie heard Kilburn thank her stiffly and heard the front door close.

Jennie came into the kitchen again. Her eyes were streaming tears. She looked at her mother, then suddenly ran to her just the way she so often had as a little girl.

Maggie held her, patting her back. Jennie wailed, "Oh Ma, what am I going to do?"

Maggie said softly, "Don't fight with him. Don't drive him away from you."

Jennie drew away and dried her eyes. Maggie wished she could offer more than that, but she could not. She turned back to her dishes, hurrying now because she was hot and tired. Her lips moved silently as she prayed that Frank Kilburn would ask Jennie to marry him. Jennie would make a good wife, a good mother. But she had to get a husband first.

IX

Ross Lockhart hadn't been exaggerating when he told Frank Kilburn that he was sick. He had the worst headache he could remember, and he felt like throwing up. Spots danced before his eyes, and he staggered when he walked. But he had no intention of going home to bed. There was too much that needed to be done.

He didn't know where Tako Nomura was. Nomura wouldn't have stayed overnight at the hotel because he had no money, and unless he had slept in an alley or shed someplace, he had probably gone home.

Lockhart staggered up the street. He stared longingly across at the Ute Saloon, but it wasn't open yet. His horse was no longer tied in front of the saloon, and he supposed someone had put the animal up at the livery.

He went into the deserted livery barn, spotting his saddle, blanket and bridle almost immediately, dumped in a pile on the floor. He picked them up and walked to the rear door, knowing his horse would be in the corral out back.

He was. Lockhart took the rope off his saddle, went into the corral and caught his horse. Moments later, he was riding north out of town, glad to have succeeded in avoiding the twenty-five cent livery stable fee for keeping his horse there overnight.

He kicked the horse into a lope because his head couldn't stand a trot. Holding unashamedly to the saddle horn, he rode up the dusty Red Creek road. After less than half a mile, he glanced back. A buggy was leaving town. He squinted his eyes and decided the man driving the buggy was Nelson Struthers. He cursed soundlessly to himself. The son-of-a-bitch! Struthers had sold all the mortgage paper on Red Creek to Adam Guthrie and hadn't even had the decency to tell people what he'd done. They'd gone on making their payments to the bank just the way they always had. Until last fall. Until they couldn't make payments anymore.

There were a couple of small, dried out ranches between town and Guthrie's place. Both had been abandoned months ago, and, Lockhart supposed, Guthrie owned them now.

At Guthrie's gate, he stopped his horse and stared angrily down the lane. Guthrie's house, a big, log structure that must contain at least a dozen rooms, stood surrounded by stately poplars, the only really green things in sight.

Being the first settler on Red Creek, Guthrie had the first water right. The entire creek now went to him, and some of it had obviously been used to keep the poplars green. Lockhart cursed angrily although he knew there was too little water left in Red Creek to irrigate anybody's hay, even if Guthrie didn't take it all.

He kicked his horse into motion again, this time permitting him to walk because the horse was sweating heavily. As he rode, he glanced occasionally at Guthrie's fields.

The hay wasn't long enough to cut, but it had been irrigated once and it now stood about eight or ten inches high. It was mostly dark green, but it was brown in the places that had missed getting water when the rest was irrigated early in the spring.

There were a couple of thousand acres

like this above Guthrie's house. And there were probably a hundred haystacks, carried over from years past. The short, uncut hay in the fields would save the lives of thousands of Red Creek cattle in the next few months. The haystacks would save thousands more. But not as long as Guthrie refused to let his neighbors' cattle in.

Scowling, angry and sick, Lockhart once more kicked his horse into a lope. A full ten miles from town, he reached the first of the small ranches on Red Creek.

This one belonged to Hattie Pomeroy. Lockhart turned his horse in at the open gate and rode down the lane toward Hattie's house.

Like Guthrie's, it was built of logs, but it wasn't nearly as large. Hattie was churning butter on the back porch. She stopped and wiped the back of a hand across her forehead as Lockhart rode into the yard.

Hattie's husband had been killed five years before in a fall from a horse. Instead of selling out and moving into town, Hattie had kept the ranch. She wore men's clothes, a man's hat and sometimes a gun. She rode with the men on the mountaintop, and she worked her ranch as efficiently as if she had been a man. In time, people stopped thinking of her as a woman. She didn't seem to mind.

She squinted now against the sun glare in the yard and said, "You look like you've been on a drunk."

Lockhart frowned. "Ute Willis like to of broke a shotgun over my head last night."

Hattie stopped churning and wiped her hands. "Get down and come on in. Jake used to say a man with a hangover needed a drink more'n he needed anything. Think you can keep one down?"

"I'll keep it down." Lockhart slid off his horse and followed Hattie gratefully inside.

She got a bottle out of one of the kitchen cupboards and poured a glass half full. She handed it to him and put the bottle back. Lockhart drank, gagged, then managed to control himself. The warmth spread through his stomach, and his head felt better almost immediately. Hattie asked, "What brings you here?"

Lockhart said, "I broke into the bank last night. I wanted to know somethin' and, by God, I found out."

Hattie studied him for a moment. She knew he wanted her to ask what he had found out, and she supposed it wouldn't hurt to humor him. She asked, "What did you find out."

"I found out who owns our mortgages. On our places and our cattle, too."

"Who?"

"Guthrie."

"*I* borrowed from the bank. The bank owns mine."

Lockhart shook his head. "Huh uh. Guthrie bought 'em all. I got into Nelson Struthers's letter file, and I found letters he had written to Guthrie and letters Guthrie had written to him. Guthrie's been buying mortgage paper for months, and now he's got it all. Mine and yours and everybody else's, too."

Hattie shrugged. "I guess that's his privilege. And I guess it's the bank's privilege to sell, although I'd think they'd tell people when they do."

"Guthrie don't want nobody to know. He intends to foreclose on every one of us, just like he did Epperson and Barney Smith. He wants to own everything from the town of Guthrie to the head of Red Creek, and if we don't stop him he'll do it, too."

"What can we do?"

"We can drive our cattle in on him, that's what. If we save our cattle, we save our ranches because even after you're foreclosed, you've still got six months to redeem. And if we can ship our cattle in the

98

fall, at least we can buy back the land. If they die, we'll have lost them and the ranches, too."

Hattie studied him a moment. "You mean you're going to cut Guthrie's fences and just drive your cattle in?"

"That's what I mean."

"He'll fight. And somebody will get killed."

"No he won't. Not if all of us do it together. We'll outnumber him two or three to one and he won't dare put up a fight."

Frowning, Hattie shook her head. Lockhart said, "You don't have to say yes or no right now. I'm callin' a meeting for tonight, up at the Hall. You be there, Hattie. Your cattle are starvin', too."

Hattie hesitated, but in the end she nodded her head. "I'll be there, Ross." Jake had always said that when you live in a community you have to be a part of it.

Ross looked longingly at the cupboard. Hattie got the bottle and poured him another drink. This one went down easier than the first. Lockhart wiped his mouth with the back of a hand. "Thanks, Hattie. See you tonight. About seven o'clock."

He went out and mounted his horse. He waved at Hattie, who stood by her churn watching him, and rode up the lane to the road.

Rufus Dillon's place was next. He gave Rufus the same message he'd given Hattie, and Rufus agreed to see the next two ranchers above his place. He gave Lockhart a drink before he left.

It was now midmorning. The heat magnified the liquor's effect on Lockhart. He was dizzy but his headache was gone.

One by one, he called on the ranchers that owned land above Guthrie's place. There were thirty of them in all. Some volunteered to notify their nearest neighbors, and Lockhart accepted their offers with gratitude.

Hugo Enzbarger's place was last. By the time he reached it, it was late afternoon and the heat was at its peak. Lockhart had consumed a lot of whiskey during the day, having been given a drink almost every place he went.

Hugo and his two sons stood in front of their house watching him approach. All three were unshaven and unkempt. All three had been drinking. Hugo growled, "What the hell do you want?"

"We're havin' a meeting at the Hall tonight. Seven o'clock."

"What for?"

Lockhart resented Enzbarger's hostility.

But he said patiently, "I broke into the bank last night to see who the hell really owns all the mortgages on the creek. It turned out to be Guthrie. He's bought 'em all and he's going to foreclose on 'em. He's already closed out Epperson and Barney Smith."

"That son-of-a-bitch hadn't better try foreclosin' me."

"That's what the meeting is about. The law says that even if he does foreclose, you still got six months to buy back your land. Thing is, if we let our cattle die, we ain't got a chance of buyin' back anything."

"So how you going to keep your cattle from dyin' off? You goin' to make it rain?"

"Huh uh. We're going to cut Guthrie's fences and drive our cattle in on him. He's got a couple thousand acres of good pasture, and he must have a hundred haystacks just sittin' there."

Enzbarger's scowl disappeared. He said, "You want a drink?"

Lockhart slid to the ground.

Enzbarger led the way into the house. Lockhart followed, and Karl and Sam came in last. Enzbarger got a bottle from the cupboard and told Karl to get glasses for all four of them.

Hugo was interested in the plan Lockhart had suggested. He was for anything that would keep his cattle from dying off. But already, his mind had seen other possibilities in the plan.

A showdown between the Red Creek ranchers and Guthrie would bring Frank Kilburn up Red Creek. The jail would be left in the care of Dan Massey, who was nowhere near as tough as Kilburn was. That would provide Hugo with a golden opportunity to break Rudy out. Rudy could leave the country, and Kilburn wouldn't dare go after him because he'd have his hands full trying to prevent a clash between the Red Creek people and Guthrie's crew.

Besides that, a showdown over Guthrie's pasture and hay might provide an opportunity to get rid of Kilburn once and for all. Hugo felt a stir of excitement at the thought.

He still remembered the feel of Kilburn's shotgun muzzle digging at the base of his skull. He remembered the cold chill of fear that shotgun had caused in him. He remembered the way his sons had berated him for letting Kilburn, single-handed, take Rudy away from them.

He gulped his whiskey and watched Lockhart finish his. He said, "We'll be there, Ross. We'll be there sure as hell."

Lockhart nodded and staggered to the

door. He climbed laboriously onto his horse and rode back up the lane toward the road.

X

At nine o'clock, even though it was dark, the heat of the day still hung in the valley of Red Creek, oppressive and still now that the wind, which had blown incessantly all day, had died.

Adam Guthrie lighted a cigar and stepped out onto the porch. He stared north toward the head of Red Creek, thinking how satisfactory it was going to be to own this valley all the way from the town of Guthrie to the head of the creek. He had been buying mortgages over the past five years; now he owned them all. Thirty of them, from Hattie Pomeroy's just to the north of his own land to Hugo Enzbarger's, at the head of the creek. All he had to do was wait. Drought would kill the cattle, and without cattle there wasn't a chance the Red Creek ranchers could pay off. Nor could they borrow the money someplace else. No one would loan money on land in this valley. Not during a year of drought.

He was sweating, and he pulled a handkerchief from his pocket and mopped his face.

A mosquito buzzed around his ear, and he turned his head and blew a mouthful of smoke at it.

Faintly he heard the pound of a horse's hooves on the road and strained his eyes, trying to see. He failed. It was too dark. But he could tell that the horse was coming from the north, and he heard the creak of the gate as the rider opened it.

Guthrie stepped quickly into the house. He took a rifle from its rack, loaded it and went back out onto the porch. Luke DesJardins had also heard the horse. He stood now by the porch steps, his revolver belted around his waist.

Neither DesJardins, who was Guthrie's foreman, nor Guthrie spoke. They simply waited as the rider pounded down the lane. The man pulled his horse to a plunging halt in front of the house and yelled excitedly, "Mr. Guthrie! Mr. Guthrie, I got to talk to you."

It was Nick Gallo, who owned a ranch about three miles up the creek. Guthrie said, "I'm here."

Gallo crossed the yard, hurrying. Reaching the porch steps, he stopped, breathing as hard as if he had been running. Guthrie asked, "What's the matter, Nick?"

"I . . . I guess I shouldn't of come." Gallo

turned and shuffled toward his horse. Guthrie said, "Wait."

Gallo stopped. Guthrie said, "You didn't ride all the way down here just to turn around and ride back. You wanted to tell me something. What was it?"

"Nothin', I guess."

Guthrie said, "It's all right, Luke. You can go back to the bunkhouse."

Luke DesJardins turned and walked away into the darkness. Guthrie said, "Come on in, Mr. Gallo. There might be a bottle of beer or two."

"Well . . ."

Guthrie turned and opened the door. He followed Gallo in, then walked swiftly to the kitchen. He got two bottles of beer out of the ice box, opened them and brought them back into the living room. Gallo was looking around in puzzlement at the bare room in which barbed wire and salt and sacks of grain were stored along with other ranch supplies. Guthrie handed him a bottle of beer. "It's cold. We've still got ice."

Gallo put the bottle to his lips and drank appreciatively. Guthrie asked, "What was it you wanted to see me about?"

"They had a meeting up at the Hall tonight. All the people on Red Creek."

"And what did they decide?"

"To cut your fences and drive their cattle in. They'll start gathering cattle as soon as it's light enough. They'll hit you sometime in the middle of the morning, or, at least, that's the way they're planning it."

Guthrie felt his chest grow tight. He asked, "Why?"

"Ross Lockhart found out you'd bought all our mortgages from the bank He said you were goin' to close us out like you did Epperson and Barney Smith."

"Why did you ride here to warn me?"

"I . . ." Gallo hesitated, cleared his throat and said doggedly, "I'm a poor man, Mr. Guthrie. I've worked mighty hard for what I got. I can't afford . . . I mean, the missus said I should come and tell you what they're goin' to do. She said you'd be grateful enough to give us more time to pay our mortgage off."

"All right. I appreciate the warning."

Gallo was silent a moment. At last, he cleared his throat and said, "Well, thanks, Mr. Guthrie. Thanks. Don't you forget now. You promised me."

"Promised you what?"

"That you'd . . . that you wouldn't . . . you said you appreciated . . ." Gallo was plainly miserable.

Guthrie said, "Thirty dollars is your price."

"What do you mean, thirty dollars? You . . ." Suddenly the meaning of what Guthrie had said sank in. Gallo said, "Damn you . . ." He turned and literally ran out the door and across the yard to his horse. He mounted and raked the horse's sides with his spurs. He pounded up the lane. Guthrie stepped out onto the porch.

Lue DesJardins materialized out of the darkness. Guthrie said, "I thought you went back to the bunkhouse."

"I changed my mind." DesJardins was silent a moment, but at last he said, "You didn't have to do that to him. He did you a favor."

"The goddamn Judas. He didn't do it for me."

"What are you going to do?"

"I don't know. Fight them off, I guess."

"Won't do. They outnumber us three to one. Not countin' women an' kids."

"We could cut loose on 'em from cover when they cut the fence."

"We could. And suppose we kill eight or ten of them? The stink from that would go all the way to the state capital."

"Go to bed. I'll think of something."

DesJardins nodded. "Good luck." There

was a wry mockery in his voice. He turned and once more disappeared.

Guthrie began to pace nervously back and forth. He hadn't wanted anyone to know that he owned the mortgages. He'd planned carefully: to close out one or two of the ranchers at a time so that there wouldn't be any mass action by those being dispossessed.

Struthers had said someone had broken into the bank last night. He'd suspected why, because nothing had been stolen and the safe had not been touched. So it had been Lockhart. Guthrie frowned.

He finished his beer and went back into the house, frowning worriedly. He had to stop the Red Creek men from cutting his fences and driving their cattle in on him. He had to stop them without letting it come to a gunfight if he could. And the only way to do that was to call on the law.

He went to the stairs and yelled, "Jess!"

He heard footsteps in the upstairs hall. His son's voice called, "What do *you* want?"

"I want you to go to town for me."

"Why?"

"Come down here and I'll tell you why." Guthrie's voice failed to conceal his irritation.

Jess came down the stairs. He was a tall

young man of twenty, and he had a bottle of whiskey in his hand. At the foot of the stairs, he raised the bottle deliberately to his mouth and took a drink, looking challengingly at his father as he did.

Guthrie said, "Damn it, put that away! I want you to go to town for me."

Jess shrugged and with deliberate slowness took another drink. Guthrie, worried and irritable anyway, knocked the bottle out of his hand with a sweep of his arm. It flew across the room and shattered against the wall. Guthrie shouted, "I said I wanted you to go to town for me!"

Jess looked straight at him. "Go yourself."

Guthrie clenched his fists in an effort at self-control. He said, "All this will belong to you someday. You ought to be willing to do a few little things for it."

"Why? Did anybody ever ask me if I wanted this?"

"I built it for you and your sister. No one else."

Jess was apparently drunk enough to be reckless. He stared straight into his father's eyes. "The hell you did! You built it for yourself. It's all you ever gave a damn about."

"I'm not going to stand here and argue with you about it. I want you to go to town.

Tell Frank Kilburn that bunch on Red Creek is coming down tomorrow to cut my fence and drive their cattle in. I want protection from the law."

Jess's eyes sneered silently. "You mean something has finally come along that you can't handle by yourself?"

Something snapped in Guthrie's mind. He swung unthinkingly. His fist collided with his son's jaw and the young man fell backward onto the stairs. He lay there, rubbing his jaw and glaring at his father with pure hatred in his eyes.

It stopped Guthrie cold, the way a dousing with ice water would. For several moments, he stood there trembling. Then he turned and headed for the door.

His daughter, Joan, had just come in. Her hair was touseled, and she was straightening her clothes. A few wisps of hay still clung to both her hair and clothes. Guthrie stalked across the room to her, white-faced and furious. He said, "You goddamn little slut. Who is it this time?"

She smiled mockingly at him. "Do you really want to know?"

He didn't want to know because knowing would mean he had to confront the man and fire him. And firing one of the hands for rolling in the hay with his daughter would heap further humiliation upon him, would further degrade him in front of his men. But he nodded dumbly.

Her smile was taunting, but in her eyes was the same hatred he had seen in the eyes of his son. She said, "It was Slim. The new one you hired two weeks ago."

"If you're lying to me . . ."

"Why should I lie? I'm already tired of him. I *want* you to fire him. Maybe the next man you get . . ."

Guthrie swung the flat of his hand. It collided with her cheek. She staggered but did not fall. Guthrie said savagely between his teeth, "You bitch! You're just like your mother was!"

She said, "And you deserved us both." Her voice was laden with contempt. She turned her head, looked at the room, and waved a hand. "Look at this! This stuff has been piled in here as long as I can remember because you're too miserly to build a storehouse for it. If you're as miserly in bed as you are in every other way, I don't blame Mother for running off with the first man she could find."

Guthrie was trembling. His heart was thumping savagely in his chest. His belly felt empty and his legs felt weak. He gasped,

"Get out of here! Get out before I kill you both!"

Neither his son nor his daughter moved. Guthrie stalked past the girl and out into the darkness of the night. Halfway between the house and the bunkhouse he stopped.

He felt dizzy and weak. He forced himself to calm. He forced his thoughts to become rational once more. He didn't want to show up at the bunkhouse looking like this.

Bleakly, he realized that Joan had deliberately baited him. She'd made no attempt to cover up. She'd wanted him to know and so had flaunted what she had done.

He felt suddenly like an old bull beset by wolves. He thought about the men on Red Creek and what they were going to do to him tomorrow. And suddenly, to his own amazement, he discovered that it didn't really seem to matter anymore.

Miserly, Joan had said. She had taunted him with the fact that his wife had run off with another man. And he'd done it all for them, for Joan and Jess . . .

He shook his head. No he hadn't. He'd done it for himself. He was the one who wanted all the land from the town of Guthrie to the head of Red Creek.

Moreover, he still wanted it. He wanted it and he'd have it, no matter who got hurt!

XI

Kilburn had no idea what time it was when a thunderous pounding on the jail door awakened him. He sat up and groped for his gun. Holding it, he crossed barefooted to the door. "Who is it?"

"It's Luke DesJardins, Frank. Open up."

Kilburn pulled back the bolt and opened the door. DesJardins was alone. Kilburn growled, "Come in," and turned toward the desk, groping for a match.

He found one, struck it, and lighted the lamp. Turning, he scratched his belly through his long underwear while simultaneously reaching for his pipe. "All right. What now?"

"The Red Creek bunch. They're comin' down tomorrow to cut Guthrie's fence. They're goin' to drive their cattle in."

"How did you find out?"

"Nick Gallo. He figured that in return for ratting on his friends he could get Guthrie to give him more time to pay his mortgage off."

Kilburn packed his pipe and lighted it. DesJardins asked, "What are you goin' to do?"

Kilburn glanced up irritably. "What I'm

paid to do, I guess. Go on home and tell Guthrie I'll do all I can."

"All you can? What kind of answer is that? Guthrie wants you to stop them from cuttin' fence. He said to tell you, if you don't, he will."

Kilburn felt his irritability stir. He was sweating and out of sorts at being awakened. He guessed the temperature must be ninety inside the jail, despite its thick stone walls. He said, "Maybe you'd better just tell him to handle it himself." He watched DesJardins closely as he spoke.

The man backtracked instantly. "Now Frank, don't be like that. We're outnumbered three to one. If we try to stop them, somebody's going to get killed."

Kilburn stared at him until DesJardins looked away. Then, in a more reasonable tone, he said, "All right. I'll be up there first thing in the morning."

DesJardins nodded. He studied Kilburn speculatively for a moment, then turned and went out into the street. Kilburn didn't move until his horse's hoofbeats had died away.

Cursing softly beneath his breath, he pulled on his pants. He'd guessed right about who owned all the Red Creek mortgages. And he had probably correctly judged

Guthrie's motives in buying them.

He finished dressing and strapped on his gun. He could hear Epperson's cot creaking. Rudy Enzbarger was snoring. He blew out the lamp, went out and locked the door behind him.

He went to the livery barn first and got his horse. Mounted, he rode out into the street and headed for Nelson Struthers's house. He didn't like the position into which he had been thrust. He didn't like being Guthrie's tool.

He dismounted at Struthers's house. After tying his horse to the banker's hitching post, he went up the walk. His boots sounded hollowly on the porch. He twisted the bell savagely half a dozen times.

Sweating in the oppressive heat, he waited impatiently. A lamp was lit upstairs, and he was able to follow its light down the stairs by looking through the opaque glass of the door. The door opened.

Nelson Struthers stood there, wearing a long, white nightshirt and holding a lamp. "Oh, it's you," he said testily.

"Uh huh. It's me."

"Well, what do you want? It had better be important."

"It's important. I want to know all about those goddamn mortgages that Guthrie has bought up."

"Who told you . . . ?"

"Never mind. Just talk. Does he own every one on Red Creek?"

Struthers nodded.

"What about the cattle loans? Does he own them?"

"He owns them, too."

"Well, why doesn't he foreclose the cattle loans? If he got their cattle, the people up there wouldn't have a chance of paying off their mortgages."

"He can't foreclose. The cattle loans aren't due."

"Why in the hell did you sell those mortgages to him anyway? You knew what he was after, didn't you?"

"I only did what any banker with any sense would do. He offered me a premium at a time when I wasn't even sure I was going to get the principal."

Kilburn turned away disgustedly. What Struthers had done was legal, even if it wasn't ethical. He heard the door close behind him, but he didn't look around.

There wasn't much to be gained now by placing blame. The damage was done. What he had to do was keep the peace.

In several ways, he thought Guthrie had bitten off more than he could chew, and he was probably realizing it tonight. He'd bought all those cattle loans and it must have driven him half out of his mind to watch cattle in which he had an interest dying for lack of feed. Kilburn grinned, thinking of the bind Guthrie had been in. If he let the Red Creek ranchers have his feed, they'd save their cattle and pay off their mortgage loans. If he didn't give them feed, the cattle would die and he would lose the money he had loaned on them. Either way, he had to lose.

He untied and mounted his horse. The first thing he needed was a posse for tomorrow. He'd handled the Enzbargers, but he couldn't handle thirty angry ranchers by himself.

He headed for Jasper Littlejohn's. He tied his horse out front and went up the walk to knock on Littlejohn's front door.

He hated waking people in the middle of the night, but he had no choice. He'd have to leave town with his posse at dawn or he'd reach Guthrie's too late to do any good.

Once more he watched the light of a lamp descend the stairs. The door opened and Jasper Littlejohn asked, "Somebody else dead, Frank?"

"No, Jasper. I need a posse. The Red Creek men are going to cut Guthrie's fence tomorrow and drive their cattle in. If I don't stop them, Guthrie will, and somebody's liable to get hurt."

"You want *me* on your posse?"

"You can shoot a gun. And it's not very far to ride."

"I've never been on a posse in my life."

"That doesn't matter, Mr. Littlejohn. Get dressed and meet me down in front of the jail in half an hour."

He started to turn away but swung back when Littlejohn said, "Wait."

Kilburn looked at the storekeeper questioningly. Littlejohn said, "I'm not going, Frank."

"Why not?"

"Those Red Creek people are my best customers. I've given them a lot of credit at the store. They need Guthrie's pasture to survive."

Kilburn frowned. "What you really mean is that you won't get your money if they're denied Guthrie's pasture and hay."

"Have it your way, Frank."

"You haven't got a choice. It's your duty as a citizen to serve on a posse if I direct you to."

"I'm not going, Frank."

"I can swear out a complaint. I can bring you into court."

118

"Then I guess that's what you'll have to do."

"Mr. Littlejohn . . ."

"Good night, Sheriff." Littlejohn firmly closed the door.

Kilburn stalked down the walk angrily. He untied his horse. He hoped Littlejohn's reaction wasn't typical of what he'd get from others when he asked.

Harve Fenway lived about a block from Littlejohn. Kilburn tried there next, but with less assurance than when he'd asked Littlejohn.

Harve owned the gun shop next to the Ute saloon. He came down the stairs carrying a lamp, worried immediately when he saw the sheriff's face. "Is something wrong down at the shop?"

"It's not that, Harve. I want you to serve on a posse. Be down at the jail at dawn with a horse and rifle."

"What's going on?"

"The Red Creek bunch is planning to cut Guthrie's fence tomorrow and run their cattle in. I've got to keep them from doing it."

Fenway frowned. "I don't know, Sheriff. I get a lot of my business from the people on Red Creek. I wouldn't want to make them mad."

Kilburn said shortly, "I wasn't asking, Harve. I was telling you. It's your duty to serve on a posse when you're asked. You haven't got a choice."

"What will you do to me if I refuse?"

"Swear out a complaint. What happens to you will be up to Judge Barngrover."

"What's the penalty?"

"Oh for Christ's sake," Kilburn said disgustedly. "Forget it." He swung around and stalked away. He could see he wasn't going to get a posse made up of the town's businessmen. But he could count on Dan Massey. And he might be able to get Sam Schell, who worked with Massey at Little-john's sawmill.

Swiftly he untied his horse, mounted and rode to Mrs. Reagan's boardinghouse. He tied and went quickly up the walk.

The front door was standing open. He went in. A lamp was burning dimly at the head of the stairs. He clicked them quietly and knocked on Dan Massey's door.

Massey was a sound sleeper, and he had to knock three times before he heard a sleepy voice inside. The floorboards creaked as Massey crossed to the door. When it opened, Kilburn said, "It's me, Dan. I need you for a posse at dawn. Bring a rifle and bring your horse."

"All right, Frank. What time is it now?"

Kilburn looked at his watch, squinting because the light was poor. "Almost four."

"Then I'd just as well stay up."

"Uh huh. Think Sam Schell would come with you?"

"Sure. I guess he would. What's going on?"

"That bunch on Red Creek is going to cut Guthrie's fence tomorrow and drive their cattle in."

"Serve the sonofabitch right if they did."

"Maybe so, but I've got to stop them anyway."

"All right. I'll be there as soon as it's light."

"Thanks." Kilburn turned and went quietly down the stairs. Two men weren't enough, but it looked like two was all he was going to get.

He rode back to the jail, his horse's hooves making a clop-clop sound in the silent street.

A lamp was burning in the kitchen of the restaurant as Jennie built up her fires and made coffee. A plume of fragrant smoke drifted from the tin stovepipe and swirled along the street. Kilburn hesitated a moment, then changed his mind about stopping and went on toward the jail.

He woke his prisoners, both of whom were

grumpy and irritable. He herded each one out of the cell to the outhouse and back again. By the time he had finished, the sky in the east was turning gray.

He walked to the restaurant and tried the door. It was locked. He knocked lightly, and a moment later Jennie opened it. "Hello, Frank. Aren't you up awfully early?"

"I need a couple of breakfasts for my prisoners," he said.

"Is something wrong?"

"I've got to leave town. The bunch on Red Creek is planning to cut Guthrie's fence."

Jennie didn't comment. She moved aside and Frank went in. He crossed to the counter and sat down. He could smell coffee, and soon Jennie brought him a cup.

He sipped it gratefully. Out in the street he heard horses' hooves and turned. Dan Massey and Sam Schell were riding across the intersection toward the jail.

It was now fairly light outside. He thought of the ride to Guthrie's upper fence and knew he had no time to wait for Jennie to cook food for his prisoners.

He took another gulp of coffee and went to the door. He yelled and saw Massey and Schell turn their horses toward him.

He went back to the counter and gulped his coffee. He called, "Jennie!"

She came from the kitchen, and he asked, "Could you feed the prisoners? I'll give you a key to the jail. All you have to do is slide the trays under the cell door."

She nodded. "I guess so. Do you have to go? Right now, I mean?"

"I'm afraid I do."

"Don't you even have time for breakfast? It won't take but a few minutes for me to fix something."

"I can't wait." He handed her the key to the front door of the jail.

She looked down at it worriedly. Kilburn asked, "Is something the matter?"

Her eyes met his. "Be careful, Frank. With only two men . . ."

He said, "I'll be all right."

She nodded dumbly. Her hands were clenched into fists at her sides. Her face was pale. She said, "Frank, about the other night . . ."

"Jennie, that's all right. We'll talk about it when I get back."

She nodded, not able to meet his glance. He turned and walked to the door. Outside in the street, Dan and Sam sat their horses, waiting for him.

Kilburn looked back at Jennie. He saw her clenched hands, her paleness, her trembling lower lip. In that instant, she looked like a little girl who has just been scolded.

He called out the door, "Dan, you and Sam go on. I'll catch up with you."

Dan nodded, and the two rode up the street. Kilburn turned back toward Jennie, knowing this had to be settled now, but not knowing what he was going to say.

XII

He looked at her uncertainly. He didn't know what he wanted to say, and he didn't know how to start. What he did know was that he'd probably botch it.

He wished it was possible to talk to a woman the way you talked to a man, in the expectation that you would be understood. But it wasn't possible because women weren't as reasonable as men. They were too liable to flare up at something they thought a man had said or meant, when he'd neither said nor meant what they thought he had at all.

Jennie looked scared, but now she looked determined, too. She had trouble meeting his glance and seemed to be defiant because of that. Kilburn felt increasingly nervous, but he said doggedly, "Why don't you fix me some breakfast, Jennie? I'll come out to the kitchen and we can talk." He knew it would help the strain between them if Jennie had something for her hands to do. Besides, he was hungry and he had a long day ahead of him.

Jennie nodded silently, turned and walked to the kitchen. Kilburn followed her. There was a stool beside the stove and he sat on it. He filled and packed his pipe, then lighted it deliberately, eyeing Jennie over the burning match. He puffed silently for several moments, watching her as she sliced bacon and put the slices into a pan. At last, he knew he had to speak. The silence was growing strained.

He said, "Jennie, about the other night . . ."

Her voice was firm, and she didn't look at him. "I don't think we had better talk about it. We'll only fight."

"Why should we fight? Besides, I thought you wanted to talk about it. That's why I stayed. I ought to be going . . ."

"And you can be, too. Nobody's stopping you."

"Jennie . . ."

"You stayed for breakfast. And I'm fixing it."

Once more the silence dragged. The bacon crisped and Jennie took it out of the pan.

She broke three eggs into the grease and put some sliced bread on a grille on top of the stove to toast.

Kilburn got uncertainly off the stool. Impatience was growing in him but he fought it down, knowing he was going to need all the diplomacy and tact of which he was capable. He crossed the kitchen to where Jennie stood.

Deliberately, she turned her back to him. He put his hands gently on her shoulders and turned her around. She winced at his touch as though it burned.

Kilburn pulled her close. "Jennie . . ." He was at a loss for the right thing to say. He hadn't had much experience with women other than the kind you found in a saloon, and he wasn't good at talking to them. Particularly in situations where there was strain.

Once more, with her so close to him, he felt the same need, the same hunger he had felt the other night. And Jennie felt it, too, because for a moment she responded, pressing against him, raising her arms to put them around his neck.

As suddenly as she had responded, she stiffened and drew back. "Oh no you don't! Not again! Just because I was foolish enough the other night to . . . Well, just because it happened once doesn't mean it's going to happen any time you want!"

"Jennie, I wasn't . . ."

She gave him no chance to finish what he had to say. Pulling free violently, she said in an angry, rising voice, "You get out of this kitchen, Frank Kilburn! You go out in front where you belong! I'll bring your breakfast, but you keep your hands off me! I might have been foolish enough once to . . . Well, maybe I was that foolish once, but I won't be again! I . . . !"

She was trembling violently and close to hysteria. Tears welled out of her eyes and streamed across her cheeks.

Frank's impatience suddenly got the best of him. He yelled, "Shut up! For once shut up, and let somebody else say what he has to say!"

Jennie's eyes widened, and she stopped speaking in the middle of a word. Her mouth was open, but she didn't seem to be aware of it.

Kilburn gave her no chance to recover. He yelled, "Damn it, you're talking us into a fight that neither of us wants!" Surprised that he had so effectively silenced her, he paused. Then he went on. "I want you to marry me! I'd have asked you a long time ago if I'd thought there was any chance you would! Maybe you won't now, but by God, you can't say you ain't been asked!"

Color had begun to return to Jennie's face, but she was still trembling. Kilburn shouted, "Well?" afraid she was going to say no, equally afraid she might say yes.

Her voice, when it came, was scarcely audible. "Frank, did you just ask me to marry you?"

"What did it sound like? Of course I asked you. All I want from you is a simple yes or no."

She nodded, her eyes wide, her glance clinging to his face. She found her voice at last and whispered, "Yes, Frank. Yes."

Kilburn suddenly began to cough, in that instant becoming aware that the kitchen was full of smoke. He glanced toward the stove and said superfluously, "It's burning."

Jennie rushed to the stove. The eggs were smoking and so was the toast. She swept the burned toast into her apron, afterward dumping it out of her apron into the coal bucket. Using a hot pad, she yanked the skillet off the stove and dumped it, too.

With that done, she turned back toward Kilburn. Something about his expression must have struck her as funny because she began to laugh. For a moment Kilburn stared, then a grin spread across his face.

Jennie ran to him and threw her arms around his neck. She kissed him firmly on the mouth. Excitedly, she said, "Sit down again, Frank, and I'll fix something else for you to eat."

Frank sat down once more on the stool beside the stove. He felt a little overwhelmed. Jennie worked swiftly, glancing often at his face.

Frank knew he ought to leave, knew he'd have trouble getting to Guthrie's place in time, but he didn't move.

When the eggs and toast were finished, Jennie put them on a plate with the bacon and carried it out front. Frank followed and sat down.

He ate as quickly as he could. Afterward, he kissed her and hurried out into the street.

His horse was still tied to the rail in front of the jail. He walked there swiftly, untied the horse, mounted and rode back up the street.

Jennie stood in front of the restaurant's open door. She was straight and smiling and radiant, and she raised a hand to wave at him.

Kilburn returned her wave, spurred his horse and galloped north out of town. He felt confused and he felt surprised. But he was pleased as well. And he couldn't help thinking ahead.

He'd need a house someplace, at the edge of town if possible. Where they could raise a lot of kids.

Jennie waited until Kilburn was out of sight. Then, hurrying, she went back into the restaurant. She took off her apron and draped it over the back of a chair. She closed the damper on the stove. Turning, she hurried out the door.

Lifting her skirts, she ran toward home. She burst into the kitchen and called excitedly, "Ma! Oh Ma, come here!"

Maggie Morgan appeared in the kitchen doorway. She knew what had happened the instant she saw her daughter's face. Jennie cried, "He asked me, Ma! He asked me to marry him! And I said yes!"

Maggie grinned at her. "I didn't expect that you'd say no."

"Isn't it wonderful? Isn't it?" Jennie's face was radiant.

"Of course it is. Of course it's wonderful. When is it going to be?"

"We didn't have time to talk about that. But I want it to be soon. Oh, I want it to be soon."

Maggie nodded, smilingly watching her daughter's face.

Jennie's face clouded suddenly. "You don't think it was because . . . ? I mean, you don't think he felt he had to because of what happened the other night?"

Maggie asked practically, "Did he act like he was being forced?"

Jennie smiled again, the worry gone. "No. He acted just like I'd always hoped he would. Ma, I'm so happy! I'm so happy I could cry."

A suspicious brightness was in Maggie's eyes. "Then cry, child. Cry."

"No. I've got to get back to the restaurant. I've got to feed his prisoners." She threw her arms around Maggie's neck. "Ma, isn't the world wonderful?"

Maggie thought of all the trouble Frank Kilburn faced. He had risked his life twice in the last week bringing in two murderers. She asked, "Where did Frank go, Jennie? You said you had to feed his prisoners."

"He had to go up Red Creek. The men up there are going to cut Guthrie's fence." Jennie hurried out the door, letting the screen slam thunderously. Maggie crossed to the door and stared after her.

Jennie was running down the sunny street like a girl without a care in the world.

Maggie hoped Jennie's world would stay carefree and wonderful. But she suddenly felt cold as she turned away from the door. She glanced up at the cloudless sky and felt the blistering heat of the morning sun. She heard the wind begin to sigh past the eaves of the house and heard it stir the browning leaves of the cottonwoods.

Heat and failure and frustration did terrible things to men. Maggie prayed wordlessly that Frank Kilburn would be safe today, but she had little faith he would.

XIII

Kilburn held his horse to a steady gallop for more than a mile. Then, because the horse was sweating profusely, he let him walk.

Already the heat was considerable. Kilburn judged it was close to a hundred degrees, and it was not yet eight o'clock. The wind was stirring, too, blowing out of the south strongly enough to whip up the dust stirred by his horse's hooves and carry it ahead.

He maintained the walk for about a quarter mile. Then, conscious that time was getting short, he spurred the horse to a gallop again.

He thought of Jennie, and a smile touched the corners of his mouth. She had promised to marry him, and he wanted it to be soon. But first he'd have to find a house. As soon as he got back to town today, he'd hire a buggy at the livery barn and take Jennie house hunting with him.

The horse began to sweat again and he let the animal walk until it cooled. Then, once more, he urged him to a lope.

Guthrie's house came into view at last. Immediately afterward, he saw the gate that opened into Guthrie's lane. A crowd of horsemen was gathered on the road beside the gate. A few moments later he drew rein short of the assembled men.

Guthrie stood out, sitting a big chestnut horse. Dan Massey and Sam Schell left the group and rode toward Kilburn. Massey said, "Guthrie insists that he's going to stop the Red Creek men, no matter what he has to do."

Kilburn said, "I'll talk to him." He rode forward, with his two deputies falling in behind.

He asked, "What's the trouble, Adam?"

"I thought you were going to bring a posse. For Christ's sake, how far do you think you're going to get with only two men besides yourself?"

"How far do you think you're going to get with ten? There will be at least thirty in the

133

Red Creek bunch."

"Well, what am I supposed to do? Just sit here and let them take my pasture and my hay?"

"I'm going to stop them. You go back to the house and take your men with you."

"*You're* going to stop them? The three of you?"

"That's what I said."

"You can't do it. It can't be done. They'll kill you and cut the fence anyway."

"I guess that's a chance we're all going to have to take."

"Well I'm not going to take that chance. Once they cut my fence and get their cattle in, I'm a ruined man."

Kilburn said firmly, "I'm giving you an order to disperse." He stared at Guthrie, puzzled by what he saw. In Guthrie, today, there was a kind of wildness that had never been apparent in the man before. Kilburn wondered what had happened to bring it out. He looked at the men behind Guthrie, from Luke DesJardins to Hughie Newman, who did the chores. All were heavily armed. Most had both rifles and handguns. Newman had a ten gauge, double-barreled shotgun.

Kilburn said, "Don't be foolish, Adam. If

you go up there, a lot of men are going to die."

"It's not my doing. I'm only protecting what belongs to me."

"That's what they're doing, too. They're trying to prevent you from taking everything they own."

"Whose side are you on, anyway?"

Kilburn shrugged. "I'm not on anybody's side. I'm trying to keep the peace."

"Then you'd better take a stand. The law says I'm in the right. The law says I've got a right to keep them from breaking in on me."

"So it does. That's why I'm here. That's why I'm going to ride up the road and stop them from cutting fence. Now go on back to the house."

Stubbornly Guthrie shook his head.

Kilburn knew his time was running out. They had reached an impasse. In a moment, Guthrie would give an order to his men and their guns would come into play. He'd have a choice of surrendering or fighting it out with Guthrie's men. Neither alternative was acceptable.

He let his shoulders slump, as though admitting defeat. He saw the gleam in Guthrie's eye.

He glanced at Massey and saw his deputy's disbelief. He didn't bother to look at

Schell, knowing Schell's expression would be the same. The horsemen behind Guthrie stirred, and Guthrie turned and raised a hand.

Kilburn moved swiftly and unexpectedly. He raked his horse's sides with his spurs and the startled animal leaped ahead. He yanked him hard right, forcing him violently against Guthrie's mount.

DesJardins yelled a wordless shout of warning to his boss, but it was too late. Kilburn threw an arm around Guthrie's neck and pulled him off his horse. He permitted himself to fall with Guthrie, and the pair hit the dust of the road simultaneously.

Kilburn released Guthrie, at the same time drawing his revolver and jamming it against Guthrie's side. He yelled, "Tell 'em! Goddamn you, tell 'em not to move or I'll blow a hole in your guts!"

Guthrie's voice came gusting out, "Hold it, boys! Hold it! The son-of-a-bitch means what he says!"

Kilburn risked a glance at the mounted men. Some had guns in their hands, but none seemed on the point of using them. He said, "Drop 'em. Drop the guns, all of you!"

There was a moment's hesitation before the guns began dropping into the road.

Most of the men leaned far over so as to minimize damage to their guns. Kilburn said, "Massey — Schell — move 'em back."

Massey and Schell rode forward, grinning triumphantly. They forced Guthrie's horsemen to back away from their guns. Kilburn dug his revolver into Guthrie's ribs again. "Stand up."

Guthrie got to his feet, dusting off his clothes. His scowl was murderous. "You're not going to get away with this. We got plenty more guns down at the house."

Kilburn said, "Schell, pick up the guns. Run a rope through the trigger guards and then tie a knot in the rope. Hang 'em over Guthrie's saddle, half on each side." He lifted Guthrie's gun out of its holster and tossed it on the ground beside those of his men.

Schell dismounted and began to gather up the guns, threading a rope through their trigger guards as he went. Guthrie stood in front of Kilburn, glowering. Schell finished, tied the rope, then lifted the bundle of guns to Guthrie's saddle, letting half hang on one side, half on the other.

Kilburn glanced at Guthrie. "Mount up."

Guthrie's face showed his dismay. "Mount up? What the hell do you mean, mount up? You're not thinking of taking me along with you, are you? Without a gun?"

"I'm taking you to town. You're under arrest."

"What for? I didn't do anything. You can't arrest a man unless he's done something."

Kilburn felt angry and irritable. Guthrie had made it impossible for him to stop the Red Creek men from cutting fence because he didn't dare take Guthrie up there with him. Nor did he dare risk sending him back with his deputies. Guthrie's men would rescue him long before they got him to town.

He said harshly, "Mount up. Unless you plan to walk." He began taking down his rope.

Guthrie said, "Luke."

Kilburn stared at Luke DesJardins. Harshly he said, "All right. Let's get this straight right now. Go ahead, Adam. Tell Luke what you want him to do."

Guthrie glared sullenly. Finally he growled, "He knows what to do."

"Does he?" Kilburn switched his glance back to DesJardins again. "What are you supposed to do? Get guns and rescue him?" He could feel his temper rising dangerously. He fumed, "Now you listen to me, the whole goddamn bunch of you! This is over, understand? If any of you try rescuing

Guthrie, he's the first one that's going to get hurt. And whoever goes up to try and fight off the Red Creek bunch will get what he deserves." He fixed DesJardins with his glance. "Is that clear to you, Luke?"

DesJardins shrugged. "I know when I'm licked."

"Good. I'm glad somebody does." He swung and stared savagely at Guthrie. "Get on that horse!"

Guthrie swung to the back of his horse, awkwardly because of all the guns hanging there. He settled himself uncomfortably. Kilburn said, "Dan, take the reins from him. Lead his horse to town."

Dan Massey rode over and took the reins out of Guthrie's hand. Guthrie's face was white with rage.

Kilburn rode south toward town without looking back. He could hear the horses of Massey, Schell and Guthrie coming along behind. He knew without looking that both Massey and Schell were grinning and that helped his disposition a little bit.

He had pulled it off. He had, at least, prevented a confrontation between Guthrie's crew and the Red Creek men.

But in a larger sense he had failed, because now there was no way he could prevent the Red Creek bunch from driving their cattle into Guthrie's fields. By the time he took Guthrie to town and returned, it would be too late. And even if he had sent Guthrie to town with Massey and Schell, it was doubtful if he alone, could have stopped them from moving in.

Behind him, Guthrie growled, "What are you going to do with me?"

Kilburn turned his head. As he had guessed, Massey and Schell were grinning, enjoying Guthrie's discomfiture. Kilburn said, "What does a sheriff do with a prisoner?"

"You're not going to put me in that stinking jail?"

"That's exactly what I'm going to do."

"With Epperson and Enzbarger?"

Kilburn asked exasperatedly, "What do you want, a private room?"

"You could put me in the hotel. I'd give you my word . . ."

Kilburn shook his head. "Maybe it'll do you good to see what the inside of a jail cell is like."

"I'll be out on bond in an hour."

"Will you? First the judge will have to find out you're there. I'm not going to tell him, and I doubt if DesJardins will."

"You can't hold me! I've got my rights."

Disgustedly Kilburn said, "For Christ's

sake, shut up! I've heard all I want to hear about your goddamn rights! What about other people's rights? You're trying to steal those ranches on Red Creek. Legally maybe, but it's still a steal, and you know it is. Now, for once in your life, stop bellyaching and take what's coming to you."

Guthrie muttered, "You'd better start looking for another job. Because, between now and the next election, I'm going to be working to make sure you don't get a single vote."

"Do that. In the meantime shut your mouth. Before I stuff a rag in it."

Sam Schell snickered, and Kilburn swung a wrathful glance at him. "And you can shut up, too!"

Schell sobered instantly.

Kilburn turned his face angrily back toward town, wondering why he'd ever gone after this job in the first place. He should have known that sooner or later it would be like this.

It was midmorning by the time he reached the town. He went immediately to the jail and unlocked the door.

Jennie had fed the prisoners. The trays were on the floor inside the cell.

He unlocked the cell door and stood aside while Guthrie was herded in. He locked it

141

again. He'd have to round up another cot before tonight. Unless Guthrie got out on bail.

He looked at Massey and Schell. "You two stick around and keep an eye on things. No visitors for any of them. I'll be back in an hour or so."

He stepped out into the blistering, sun-baked street. He headed for the livery barn to hire a buggy.

He knew he'd be criticized for going house hunting while the Red Creek men were cutting Guthrie's fence. He discovered he didn't give a damn. He'd tried to get help from the responsible men in town, and he'd been turned down by everyone he'd asked.

XIV

The meeting at the Red Creek Community Hall had been stormy and long. For hours, the Red Creek ranchers argued bitterly about what should be done.

Lockhart got up repeatedly to tell them what he had discovered at the bank and what he thought they ought to do. It was simple he said, and he didn't know what all the argument was about. Guthrie was try-ing to get their ranches by foreclosing the mortgages he had purchased from the bank. The only way they could circumvent him was by keeping their cattle alive so that they could be shipped to Denver in the fall. Selling them would provide the money needed to make the payments on Guthrie's mortgages. And since Guthrie had the only feed left on the entire creek, cutting his fences was the only possible way of keeping the cattle from starving to death.

It was past midnight before the matter came to a vote. The result was overwhelming if not unanimous. Twenty five of the Red Creek families voted to cut Guthrie's fence. Four voted against it. One was absent from the meeting.

The meeting broke up almost immediately after the vote, with the men promising to meet at dawn the next day at the Hall. Their wives and sons were to start gathering cattle simultaneously, driving them toward Guthrie's fence, which would have been cut by the men long before the cattle herd arrived.

Lockhart rode home immediately after the meeting. His head still ached, probably from the blow Ute Willis had struck the night before. He felt dizzy and a little drunk.

But he felt triumphant, too. He had done what he had set out to do. The Red Creek men were going to cut Guthrie's fence. They were going to drive their cattle in. At least the cattle wouldn't die, and if they did not, they could be sold in the fall and the mortgage payments met.

He didn't bother to light a lamp. Nor did he take off his clothes. He lay down on the bed and promptly went to sleep. He did not awaken until his customary rising time, half an hour before dawn. He hadn't seen Nomura last night and he didn't see him now. He supposed Nomura had deserted him.

He staggered out to the pump and let a stream of cold water run over his head. He felt dizzy, but it was not until gray began to streak the eastern sky that he discovered he was seeing double.

It worried him, but he knew he couldn't go back to bed. Today was too important. He rummaged around until he found a bottle that was half-full of whiskey. He took a big drink from it. Feeling a little better, he went out to saddle up his horse.

Ten minutes later, further fortified with whiskey, he rode up to the road. He met the group of ranchers riding south a mile above his gate.

They hailed him boisterously, and he fell in and rode with them. They were traveling at a steady trot. Hugo Enzbarger called, "Ross, I told my boys to see your cattle got gathered up."

Lockhart nodded his thanks. That motion and the movement of his trotting horse made his head hurt even worse. He stared at the man ahead of him, seeing double images. He swayed and caught himself by grabbing the saddle horn.

Damn! This was a hell of a time to be feeling bad. But maybe later on today he could ride into town and get Doc Peabody to give him something for his head.

The sky grew lighter and at last the sun came up. The group grew larger with every passing mile. They reached Guthrie's upper fence at seven o'clock.

Here, trees and thick brush lined the creek. The group halted and milled uncertainly, staring toward the creek. Enzbarger said, "Looks like we caught the bastard by surprise."

Lockhart shook his head. "Don't count on it. He could be down there in them trees just waitin' for us to cut his fence."

A man yelled, "Then let's not disappoint the sonofabitch!"

The group had no leader as such. Lockhart stepped into the breach. He yelled, ignoring his pounding head. "Those with wire cutters get down and get busy. Cut every wire between every post. Some of you others yank the posts out with your ropes as soon as the wire has been cut. We ought to take out a mile of fence along the road. Enough so's he can't put it back as soon as we're out of sight."

There were the sounds of wire being cut. Men roped fence posts and dallied the rope ends around their saddle horns. Spurring their horses, they yanked out the posts and dragged them above the road into the brush.

Lockhart continued to stare toward the trees that lined the creek. No movements were visible. No shots broke the morning stillness.

He shook his head, trying to clear the double vision, but he failed. He only made his head ache worse.

Tearing out a mile long section of fence took less than half an hour. Lockhart noticed Nick Gallo sitting his horse well away from the group guarding those who were tearing out the fence and rode to him. "What's the matter, Nick? You look scared."

Gallo couldn't meet his eyes. "Is he going to let us cut his fence? Ain't he going to do anything?"

"He don't know about it, Nick. That's why he ain't here."

Gallo agreed, "No. I guess he don't." But

he kept watching the tree-lined creek nervously.

"You just going to sit there? Ain't you going to help?"

"I don't see you doing anything."

"No, but I got a gun in my hands. I'll do something if Guthrie and his men show up. What will you do, Nick? Run?"

"Maybe. Maybe we all ought to run. This is too damn easy, Ross. The sonofabitch has probably got an ambush waiting down there for us."

"How can he, when he don't even know we're here?"

"I wouldn't bet that he don't know. Guthrie knows everything that's goin' on."

"How could he know? Unless somebody told him?"

"How should I know?"

"Did you tell him, Nick?"

Gallo's face looked gray. He couldn't seem to raise his glance. Ross said, "Why don't you look at me?"

Again Gallo tried desperately to raise his glance. Briefly he succeeded. His glance met Lockhart's and immediately slid away. Lockhart breathed, "Why you dirty sonofabitch! You did tell Guthrie, didn't you?"

"I didn't! I swear I didn't! Why would I tell on you?"

Lockhart's head was aching horribly. The glare of the merciless sun only made it worse. He was sweating, and he felt like he was going to be sick. But it gave him savage pleasure to turn his head and yell, "Boys, what do you know? Nick rode down to Guthrie's last night and told him what we were goin' to do. That's why he's been hangin' back the way he has. That's why he's afraid that Guthrie's got an ambush waiting someplace for us."

A dozen of the men surrounded Gallo, their faces cold and hard. One of the men said, "Why don't you deny it, Nick?"

Gallo looked up, panic in his eyes. He looked from one hard face to the next. "I do deny it. Lockhart just made it up."

"Then you ride ahead of us. If you didn't tell Guthrie we were comin', I don't see how he could know."

Gallo's fear fought with his sense of guilt. He nodded dumbly. The others moved their horses around behind his, forcing him to ride ahead. Those who had been cutting fence mounted and fell in behind. The entire group moved slowly down the road toward Guthrie's gate.

Gallo turned his head. "Where you goin' now? I thought you was just goin' to cut Guthrie's fence."

For a moment no answer to that question was forthcoming. But Lockhart, with his fiercely aching head, felt mean. He yelled, "Do? Why hell, there ain't no use in quittin' now! We got him buffaloed or he'd of been here with his crew. I say let's teach the son-of-a-bitch a thing or two. Let's burn him out. Let's show him how it feels to lose everything you got!"

His suggestion was greeted immediately by enthusiastic shouts. Someone spurred his horse into a gallop and the others followed suit. The group of nearly thirty thundered down the road, raising a cloud of dust that the wind whirled and raised to a height of fifty feet.

Lockhart stayed in the saddle only by clinging desperately to his saddle horn. It took the group thirty minutes at full gallop to reach Guthrie's gate. One of them opened it. Leaving it open, they thundered down the lane toward Guthrie's house.

Luke DesJardins and the crew came out of the bunkhouse and stood in the yard, hands raised in the air. It was a good thing for them they did. The Red Creek men were, by now, completely out of control. In Guthrie's ranch they had found an outlet for all the months of frustration caused by drought, by heat, by helplessness at watching their cattle die.

Not a one regretted cutting Guthrie's fence. Not a one hung back from what they had come here to do.

Someone found a can of coal oil in a shed. He poured a trail of it through the house, came out and dropped a match where the trail began. Flame licked up, crawling along the coal oil trail through the entire lower floor.

Guthrie's son and daughter came running out, to be seized by the Red Creek men. Neither put up any resistance, and both stood and watched the fire inside the house and the one that had been kindled in the barn grow until the heat forced everyone to pull back to the edge of the yard.

Before the bunkhouse was fired, Hugo Enzbarger yelled, "DesJardins, you and the others go in and get your stuff!"

DesJardins and the others hurried into the bunkhouse. They came out moments later, carrying their things. Enzbarger yelled, "Go down to the corral and saddle up. Ride out of here and don't come back. If we see any of you on Red Creek after today, you'll be shot on sight!"

A howl from the others gave emphasis to his words. DesJardins and the rest of Guthrie's crew hurried to the corral and caught horses for themselves. They mounted and rode out quickly, heading for town, glad to get away.

Lockhart felt sicker than ever before in his life. The world was whirling crazily. The strength of his hands was hardly enough to hold him on his horse.

The bunkhouse caught. Smoke poured from its broken windows and from its open door. By now, the house had sent a column of smoke five hundred feet into the air. It trailed upstream for two miles, carried away on the hot wind blowing out of the south.

Enzbarger glanced at Lockhart. "You look like hell."

"I feel like hell. I think I'd better get into town and see Doc Peabody. Maybe he can give me something."

Enzbarger stared at the faces of the Red Creek men. They were flushed and shining with sweat. But their eyes held excitement and a new kind of wildness, and he knew they could be used to free his son.

He yelled, "Now what? You ain't going to quit now, are you?"

Someone shouted in reply, "What else is there to do?"

"Why get them goddamn mortgages, that's what! Let's go on into town and get 'em from the bank. They'll make a prettier

151

fire than this, I can tell you that!"

The suggestion caught on immediately. One man yelled, "What about Frank Kilburn?" but he was shouted down. Leaving the fires burning unchecked, leaving Guthrie's son and daughter there in the yard, the mob of Red Creek men galloped up the lane to the country road.

Grimly determined, they turned toward town. Lockhart clung to his saddle horn, lagging toward the rear. Hugo Enzbarger, having taken over Lockhart's position of leadership, rode at the column's head.

His eyes, narrowed against the glare, gleamed. His mouth was set in a thin, hard line. When the mob invaded the bank, Frank Kilburn would have to try to make them leave. Nobody would know who fired the shot that cut Frank Kilburn down.

With the sheriff dead, no one would worry about guarding his prisoners. And once released, Rudy could get out of the country. He could be a couple of hundred miles away before anybody got around to going after him.

Enzbarger held his horse to a steady gallop. He knew it was essential that they reach town as soon as possible, before Kilburn, having seen the smoke, had time to organize a posse of the men in town.

XV

In a rented buggy, Kilburn drove out of the livery barn. The top shielded him from the direct rays of the sun, but the temperature was well over a hundred degrees.

Jennie was waiting for him at the restaurant. She came out, perspiring, but smiling with pleasure, and he helped her to the buggy seat. Then he climbed in after her and clucked to the horse. "Know of any houses that are for rent?" he asked.

"The McKinney house is vacant. So is the Wilberforce place."

"Which one do you like best?" He knew both houses. The McKinney house was the smaller of the two, a one-story frame, with white paint peeling from weather, and the yard dried up and gone to seed. The Wilberforce house was bigger and in better shape, but it had also been vacant for a long time.

"Let's look at both of them." Her face was excited and her eyes shone. He grinned, put an arm around her shoulders and hugged her.

He drove down Main Street, past the gun shop, the Ute Saloon and Littlejohn's Mercantile. By the lumberyard he turned right, went a block, then drew the buggy to a halt.

The McKinney house sat on the corner, backed up against the bed of Red Creek. A bridge, narrow and rickety, spanned the creek just beyond, and giant cottonwoods shaded house and yard and the creek behind the house.

Kilburn helped Jennie down, thinking that he'd passed this house fifty or a hundred times in the last year without ever really noticing it until right now.

Jennie pushed open the sagging gate and walked through the high weeds of the yard. Kilburn followed, thinking of little boys, happy with this yard and the whole of Red Creek to play in.

Jennie went from window to window, scrubbing a spot clean with the heel of her hand at each one so that she could see inside. Having looked in all of them, she turned. "I like it. I can hardly wait . . ." She stopped and flushed embarrassedly.

He grinned. "I can hardly wait, too. When is it going to be, Jen?"

"Two weeks? Is that too soon?"

"Too long. But it will give me time to fix up this place." He went up on the porch and read the typewritten notice tacked to the front door. It said that prospective renters should contact Ed Burke, Attorney at Law, in the Guthrie Bank Building.

Jennie was excited and it showed. "Take me home, Frank. I've got a million things to do."

"Will I see you tonight?"

"Of course. I'll try to get off early."

He helped her into the buggy, climbed up after her, and slapped the horse's back with the reins. The horse trotted away. Kilburn turned the corner, but not before he had noticed a column of smoke several miles away up the valley of Red Creek.

He didn't mention it to Jennie, who was chattering excitedly about all the things she had to do, but his smile was forced. Jennie apparently didn't notice, though, because her excited chattering went on.

Kilburn turned into First Street, with a quick glance over his shoulder at the column of smoke. It was higher than when he had first noticed it, blowing north on the stiff south wind. He judged it was coming from Guthrie's place. He hoped it was a haystack, but the smoke did not seem dense enough for that. Guthrie's barn or house, he guessed. The Red Creek men hadn't been satisfied with cutting fence. They had fired one or more of Guthrie's buildings. And having done so, they would be coming on to town.

He turned his head and looked at Jennie, still chattering animatedly. "Where do you want me to drop you off? At home?"

"What time is it?"

He looked at his watch. "11:30."

"Better take me to the restaurant. Ma will need some help."

As he helped her down in front of the restaurant, he glanced worriedly north up First Street. No riders were in sight. Jennie went into the restaurant, and Kilburn turned the buggy around and headed for the livery barn.

He left it there and hurried out into the street again. Once more he glanced up First Street, relieved that no riders were in sight.

Nelson Struthers was standing on the walk in front of the bank, looking up the valley of Red Creek. He saw Kilburn and said, "That's quite a fire. I wonder what it is."

Kilburn said, "Guthrie's house and barn would be my guess."

"Aren't you going to do anything?"

"What would you suggest?"

"You could go up there and find out. Buildings don't just burn by themselves. Somebody has to set them."

"Who do you think set Guthrie's buildings?"

"The Red Creek bunch. And if they did, they'll be coming on to town." Struthers looked scared. "I want protection from them, Frank. No telling what they'll do. If they're crazy enough to cut Guthrie's fence and set fire to his buildings, they're crazy enough to loot the bank."

Kilburn said, "I tried to raise a posse. Nobody wanted to serve on it."

"Well, try again. I'm entitled to protection from the law."

"Will you serve on it?"

Struthers didn't even hesitate. "No, sir! I haven't fired a gun in twenty years."

Kilburn shrugged. "You see?" Ed Burke came down the outside stairway that led to his office over the bank. He looked north, then glanced at Kilburn's face. "What's all the smoke?"

"Fire on Guthrie's place, I think. Set by the men that live on Red Creek. I need a posse, Ed. I figure they'll be coming into town."

"How many men you got?"

"Two. Dan Massey and Sammy Schell."

"That's all?"

"You'll make three. I'll get some more."

Burke shook his head. "You get some

more first. There are thirty men up there on Red Creek, and Enzbarger is one of them. I'll help, but I'm not a fool."

Kilburn nodded. He had expected this. He said, "I want to rent the McKinney house."

Burke studied him. "Well I'll be damned. You and Jennie?"

Kilburn nodded. "How much is the rent?"

"Twelve and a half a month."

Kilburn dug in his pocket. He found a ten dollar gold piece, two silver dollars and a half. He gave them to Burke. "I'll be in there doing some work as soon as things quiet down. Will you drop the key off at the jail?"

"Sure." Ed Burke turned and slowly went back up the stairs.

A couple of men came from the direction of the saloon, headed for the bank. Kilburn stopped them before they could go inside. "I need a posse, boys. I want you both to serve on it. Go on down to the jail and wait for me."

One, Jonas Brunner, who drove the mail stage up Red Creek, asked, "What's all the smoke?"

"Guthrie's buildings, probably."

Brunner said, "I ain't got time to serve on no posse, Frank. I got to take the mail on up the creek."

Kilburn looked at his companion, Jack Farley, a teamster for the Junction City Freight Company. "What about you, Jack?"

Farley shook his head. "I got to get back down the river with my rig. The boss'll skin me if I ain't in Junction City before it gets dark tonight."

Both men went into the bank. Kilburn glanced at Struthers. "You see? I asked four men and got turned down four times. It was the same way yesterday."

"What are you going to do?"

"I'm going back down to the jail."

"You can't just leave! You know they'll be coming here!"

Kilburn looked at him disgustedly, then turned and walked away. It was almost noon.

Kilburn went into the jail, bolted the door and sat down in his swivel chair. From where he sat, he could plainly see the column of smoke on Red Creek several miles away. It seemed to have thinned. Guthrie's buildings were probably almost consumed.

He was beginning to get a little scared. If the men on Red Creek would cut Guthrie's fence and burn him out, they were capable of looting the bank to get their mortgages.

But it wasn't only this that worried him. Property that has been destroyed can be restored.

What really worried him was that the mob would eventually come after Guthrie himself. With Lockhart and Enzbarger to egg them on, they might try getting Guthrie out of jail so they could tar and feather him or string him up.

In addition, Hugo Enzbarger had a personal stake in wanting the jail attacked. He'd want to get Rudy out. He'd want to give Rudy a chance to get away.

Kilburn put his feet up on the desk, packed and lit his pipe. Back in the cell, Guthrie called, "How long do you think you're going to keep me? Does Judge Barngrover know I'm here?"

Kilburn said, "I don't know. I haven't told him."

"Well, I want a lawyer. I'm entitled to one. You can't hold me without accusing me of a crime."

Kilburn did not reply. Guthrie called, "You hear me? I want a lawyer and I want him now!"

"Who do you want?"

"Ed Burke. Who else? There ain't but one lawyer besides John Gardell in town."

"I'll tell him next time I see him. In the

160

meantime, shut up. You're making too much noise."

Guthrie came to the bars and stared past Kilburn into the street. Kilburn hoped he wouldn't see the smoke, but apparently he did. He asked, "What's all the smoke?"

"I don't know."

"It looks like . . . Hell, that smoke is coming from about where my place is."

"Looks like it."

"Ain't you going to do anything? You just going to sit there on your butt?"

"What do you think I ought to do?" Kilburn was getting angry now. Everybody wanted to tell him what to do, but nobody wanted to give him any help.

"Go up there and find out what it is. If they've set fire to my barn or house . . . by God, I'll prosecute. I'll see that every one of those bastards goes to jail!"

"That's your privilege. In the meantime, whatever is burning, well, it's gone."

"My kids! They might've been in the house!"

Kilburn shook his head. "Those neighbors of yours might burn up property, but they're not murderers. They wouldn't hurt your kids."

"Maybe they didn't know . . ." Guthrie stopped a moment. "Jess might've been asleep. You know how much he drinks."

Kilburn said, "I'm sorry, Adam, but it's too late. It was too late by the time I saw the smoke."

For several moments, Guthrie was silent. "You think they might come to town?"

"They might."

"You think they might make Struthers give them the mortgages?"

"It's possible." Kilburn studied him. "They also might come here. I'm not trying to scare you, but I think you ought to know what we're up against."

"Well, go out and get some help! Don't just sit there waiting for them to come!"

Someone knocked on the jail door. Kilburn crossed to it and opened it. Judge Barngrover stood outside on the walk. "I hear you've got Adam Guthrie in jail."

"Yes sir, I have."

"Why? What did he do?"

"Nothing. Arresting him was the only way to stop him from starting a gunfight with his neighbors up on the creek."

"You'll have to turn him loose."

Kilburn shook his head. "Turning him loose would be like killing him. The Red Creek bunch has cut his fence and burned his buildings, and I don't think they're going to be willing to stop at that. Keeping

Guthrie in jail is the only way I can keep him safe. I'm not even sure he's safe in here."

"Maybe if you'd release him, he'd get out of town. Struthers is getting ready to go." The judge looked at Guthrie. "Will you leave if we turn you loose?"

"No, by God, I won't!"

"Then I guess you'll have to stay. At least until things calm down." The judge looked at Kilburn again. "How many men have you got?"

"Two. I've asked others but they turned me down."

Barngrover seemed to expect that answer. He put his hand on the doorknob. "I'll talk to those Red Creek men when they get to town. This insanity has got to stop."

"I wish you luck. But don't expect too much. This has been coming for a long, long time. Insanity is what it is — brought on by this damn heat and drought. But Guthrie made it worse by trying to take their homes away from them."

Guthrie growled, "It was legal. Everything I did."

Kilburn didn't answer him. The judge went out.

Massey and Schell, looking worried, stood at the windows looking out. After a while,

Massey said, "There goes Struthers, heading for Junction City with his wife."

That left the bank unguarded. Kilburn got to his feet. "I'm going up to the bank. Keep the door barred and don't let anybody in."

He went out into the furnace heat of the street and walked slowly toward the bank. He didn't know whether he could stop them or not but he knew he had to try. If he could stop them at the bank, maybe he wouldn't have to confront them at the jail.

XVI

They came sweeping into town at a steady gallop, raising a pillar of dust that obscured everything behind them and made them seem to be advancing out of a cloud. The thunder of their horses' hooves drew the gaze of everyone in the street. In front of the bank, they drew their plunging horses to a halt.

Hugo Enzbarger's great bulk seemed to dwarf his horse. Ross Lockhart clung to his saddle horn, swaying precariously. Kilburn thought it was pretty early for him to be so drunk.

He judged there must be close to thirty men in the milling group. Enzbarger's voice rose over the confusion in a bull-like roar, "Move aside, Kilburn! We're goin' in the bank!"

Spread legged, Kilburn stood directly in front of the locked door of the bank. He had noticed earlier that the shades had been drawn by Struthers before he left. He said, "It's closed!"

"What do you mean, it's closed?"

"Nelson Struthers went to Junction City on business."

Enzbarger laughed. "I'll bet he did! The business of savin' his stinkin' hide!"

Lockhart found his voice. "Move aside, Kilburn. We're goin' in the bank after those mortgages!"

Kilburn said, "Won't do you any good. They're all on record at the courthouse."

Enzbarger roared, "Then we'll go to the courthouse, too!"

Kilburn shook his head. "You'll have to go over me."

That sobered them for an instant, but only for an instant. Enzbarger yelled, "Then, by God, it'll have to be over you!"

Kilburn saw Hattie Pomeroy in the crowd. "What are you doing here, Hattie?"

At first, she was silent. Then she said resentfully, "Same as the others, Frank. It's fight or lose everything."

"Does fighting include burning a man's house and barn?"

She flushed. "I didn't favor that."

"But you were there."

She stared at him sullenly. He said, "Go home, all of you. Guthrie is in jail."

"What good is that going to do?" someone asked.

Kilburn didn't answer that. Enzbarger roared, "Talk ain't getting us nowhere! I say let's go in the bank. After that, let's go to the courthouse and burn the book those mortgages are recorded in."

Kilburn drew his gun. "I can get five of you!"

"But you won't!" Enzbarger heeled his horse across the walk. The animal's shoulder pinned Kilburn against the door of the bank. Enzbarger, with his right side shielded from the view of the others, shoved his revolver against Kilburn's head. He breathed, "Now then, you son-of-a-bitch . . . !"

Kilburn held his breath. There was a sudden commotion just behind Enzbarger. The milling riders pulled away from it. Kilburn couldn't see what it was, but the pullback left Enzbarger isolated and alone. The man's gun muzzle was withdrawn from his head, and Enzbarger's horse danced away.

Kilburn discovered that he was drenched with sweat. His hands were shaking violently. Never before in his life had he been so close to death.

Beyond Enzbarger, Ross Lockhart lay motionless in the dusty street. Kilburn crossed to him and knelt. Lockhart's face was gray, a ghastly color Kilburn didn't associate with drunkenness. He could detect no movement in Lockhart's chest. He picked up the prone man's wrist.

There was no pulse. He glanced up. "Ross is dead."

"Dead? What do you mean, he's dead? Is this some kind of trick?"

Kilburn said, "No trick. Somebody get Doc Peabody."

"How could he be dead? What killed him?"

"I don't know. Ute Willis hit him on the head with a gun stock the other night. Maybe that was it."

In the face of death, most of the Red Creek men were shocked, silent and motionless. Enzbarger was not, but Kilburn didn't notice him until it was too late. The loop of Enzbarger's rope settled over his head and tightened savagely. He was yanked away from Lockhart's body as Enzbarger spurred his horse. Helplessly, he was dragged

167

through the deep dust of the street, dragged across the intersection and down the street to the jail.

He fought to get his hands on his gun. The motion stopped and he saw Enzbarger above him, looking down, a wicked gleam in his narrow-set, piglike eyes. He knew if he touched the butt of his gun, Enzbarger would kill him where he lay. He forced his hand to relax, to fall away from the gun.

Enzbarger slacked the loop and shook it off. He whirled his horse and spurred away up the street.

Kilburn, struggling to his feet, heard the tinkle of breaking glass. He couldn't see the door of the bank because of all the horses and men in front of it, but he didn't have to see it to know what was happening. Behind him, the jail door opened and Dan Massey came out onto the walk. Schell followed him. Both men had shotguns in their hands. Massey said apologetically, "Frank, we'd have butted in, but we wasn't sure you'd want us to."

Kilburn said, "Glad you didn't. All Enzbarger needed was an excuse."

"What are they doin'?"

"Breaking into the bank. They want their mortgages. When they get them, they're going to the courthouse after the book they're recorded in."

"You going to stop them?"

Kilburn shook his head.

Massey stared at him in puzzlement. "Why not?"

"I'd just as soon not have anybody else get killed." He saw Doc Peabody cross the intersection, following two men who were carrying Lockhart's body toward the hotel veranda, where there was some shade. He said, "You two go on back inside. Lock the door and keep those shotguns handy. Don't let anybody in but me."

Both men withdrew into the jail. Kilburn heard the bolt shoved into place.

He walked along the street to the hotel, staying close to the building fronts so that he could remain in the shade. He wanted to talk to Doc Peabody. He wanted to know the exact cause of Lockhart's death.

Lockhart's body had been laid on one of the long settees on the hotel veranda. Doc had pulled a chair close and was looking into Lockhart's open eyes. He glanced up as Kilburn climbed the veranda steps. "Looks like Ute hit him harder than I thought."

"That's what I wanted to talk to you about. I want to know what you're going to put on the death certificate."

Doc said, "Right now I'd say fractured skull. I thought it was only a concussion, but it looks like I was wrong."

"Would it have made any difference?"

"Maybe. If Ross bad gone to bed, it might have saved his life." He shrugged. "Then again, maybe not."

"He wouldn't have gone to bed, unless I'd kept him in jail, and I had nothing to hold him on."

"Why wouldn't he?" Kilburn could see Doc was blaming himself for incorrectly diagnosing Lockhart's injury.

"He'd broken into the back door of the bank the night before. He knew Guthrie owned the Red Creek mortgages. Nothing could have kept him from riding up the creek to tell everybody what he'd found out."

"I wish I could feel sure of that."

"You can. How soon can you tell me for sure that Ute's blow was what killed Ross?"

"Couple of hours."

Half a dozen townsmen were scurrying past the hotel on their way to the jail, having carefully avoided the milling horses and men in front of the bank. One was Jasper Littlejohn. Another was Judge Barngrover. Littlejohn saw Kilburn on the veranda and stopped. "Aren't you going to stop them,

Frank? They're inside the bank. They broke the door glass to get in."

"I tried stopping them. Short of shooting somebody, it wasn't possible."

"Then shoot some of them. Hell, man, you're supposed to enforce the law and they're breaking it."

Kilburn felt anger rising recklessly in his mind, but he kept his voice even as he said, "If I'd been able to get up a posse, maybe this wouldn't be happening. But none of you would help, remember?"

Littlejohn flushed, but he persisted stubbornly, "That's got nothing to do with it. You're the sheriff. You're the one who's supposed to enforce the law. Go over there and shoot some of them if that's what it takes to get them out of the bank."

Kilburn shook his head, trying hard to keep his temper checked.

"Why not? For God's sake, why not? Are you afraid?"

Kilburn said, "Those are law-abiding men over there in the bank. This is the first time they've ever broken the law, and it will probably be the last. They're not going anywhere. They'll be called to account for what they do today. But I'm not going over there and start executing them just because the heat and drought have driven them to do this.

Now, if you'll stop meddling in my business, maybe you can take care of yours, Mr. Littlejohn. There's a dead man here. I'd suggest you hitch a team to your hearse and come after him."

Littlejohn seemed about to speak again. He changed his mind, turned and stalked angrily down the street.

Judge Barngrover remained on the walk for a moment with the other men. He also seemed about to speak, but changed his mind under Kilburn's smoldering stare. He turned and stalked away toward the courthouse, the others following sullenly. Doc Peabody grinned. "They want law and order, but not if they have to dirty their own hands providing it."

Kilburn nodded.

"If you can use an old broken-down sawbones, I'd be glad to help. After I finish doing an autopsy on Ross."

Kilburn said, "I can use all the help that's offered me. Even from a broken-down old sawbones. Come up to the jail as soon as you get through."

He stepped down off the veranda and headed back toward the jail. There was a lot of yelling over in front of the bank. He tried not to pay any attention to it, even though every instinct demanded that he go over there and stop what was going on.

He reached the jail and knocked. Massey peered out the window, saw who it was and unlocked the door. Kilburn went inside.

It was cool inside the jail. Kilburn walked to the window and stared gloomily at the mob in front of the bank. He couldn't down his feeling of uneasiness. It was as though he sensed that breaking into the bank would only whet the appetite of the mob.

As he watched, they mounted their horses. Leaving the bank, they thundered up the street toward the courthouse, almost riding Judge Barngrover down.

Massey asked, "What are they up to now?"

"I told them there wasn't any use in getting the mortgages out of the bank because they were recorded at the courthouse. They're going to get the book they're recorded in and burn it, too."

"And then what?"

Massey had asked the question that had been tormenting Kilburn ever since the mob rode into town. They had cut Guthrie's fences and burned him out. They had raided the bank, and they were about to raid the courthouse. No one knew better than Kilburn how violence begets more violence. The Red Creek men wouldn't quit when the record book and mortgages were destroyed. The temperature in the street was 110°. Months of heat and drought and fear and frustration were driving these men to what they did. Burning mortgages and record books wouldn't ease their need to act, so long suppressed. But where would they turn next?

They'd come to the jail for Guthrie, he supposed. Enzbarger would put that into their heads because Enzbarger wanted the jail door broken down. He wanted Rudy out. A long prison term awaited Rudy if he ever went to trial.

Back in the cell, Epperson called, "How about somethin' cold to drink? And how about dinner? I'm getting hungry as hell!"

Kilburn said, "You'll have to wait." All of them would have to wait. The mob had the initiative.

He had refused to shoot normally law-abiding men in defense of the bank, or even in defense of the courthouse record books. But they weren't going to get Guthrie away from him. No matter what he had to do, he meant to hold his prisoners.

XVII

There was no resistance at the courthouse.

174

Ernie Contreras, the deputy county clerk and recorder, surrendered the record book immediately upon Hugo Enzbarger's request. He protested feebly when Enzbarger started out of the room with it, but his protest died as Enzbarger swung back, pointing his rifle and scowling ferociously.

Carrying the bulky book, Enzbarger pushed through the crowd of men in the courthouse hall. Once he growled, "Goddamn Mexican!" even though Ernie had done nothing but what Enzbarger had told him to.

In the street in front of the courthouse he flung the book down into the dust. "Let's have a little bonfire, boys."

A couple of the men squatted and started tearing the pages out of the book. Someone else struck a match and lit the pile. One or two, including Hattie Pomeroy, hung back, looking worriedly toward Judge Barngrover, who was watching from the courthouse steps.

The fire burned high for a few minutes, but eventually it died. That was a letdown for the men. They looked at each other, as if wondering what they should do next.

Enzbarger knew that if let alone, they would probably disperse. He yelled, "I'll stand the drinks, boys! Come on down to the saloon!"

That perked them up. They mounted their horses and followed Enzbarger to the saloon, yelling noisily. They dismounted and trooped inside.

Enzbarger shouted at Ute Willis to give everybody a drink. They lined the bar, some drinking beer, some whiskey. Enzbarger bawled, "Hell, Ute, give 'em another one!"

The noise inside the saloon increased. Enzbarger bought yet another drink. In the heat, three was enough to make men, most of whom hadn't had a drink in months, a little drunk. Enzbarger stood at the end of the bar and yelled, "We done a good day's work, boys, but we ought to finish her."

A man yelled, "What d'you mean, Hugo?"

"We fixed Guthrie, by God, but we ain't got rid of that Mexican sonofabitch an' his stinkin', wooly sheep! An' I'll tell you this. Leave him be an' he'll do just what Guthrie tried to do. He'll run us all off Red Creek. He'll run us off the mountain. Cattle won't graze where sheep have been. Hell, they won't even drink where a goddamn sheep has drunk!"

"Whatdaya think we oughta do to 'em?"

"We ought to string the bastards up! But then, maybe that's too much. How about tar an' feathers an' runnin' 'em out of town on a goddamn rail?"

"Where are they? Are they in town?"

"I seen 'em go into the restaurant no more'n half an hour ago!"

"How about another drink first, Hugo?"

"Sure, boys! Give 'em another drink, Ute. Hell, man, give 'em two!" He slammed a handful of gold coins down on the bar. Ute looked at them and began to pour the drinks.

While the others had been getting the mortgages in the bank, Hugo had been busy getting cash. These gold coins were part of it. The paper money he intended to give to Rudy to help him get away.

But first he had to get Rudy out of jail. And before he could, he had to get Frank Kilburn and his two deputies away from it. He took another drink himself. Then he waited, knowing the more the men had to drink the more manageable they would be.

Kilburn saw the mob go into the Ute Saloon. He heard Hugo Enzbarger bellowing and knew Enzbarger was trying to incite them into doing something else.

What it could be, he had no idea. But he knew he'd better find out so that when it happened it wouldn't catch him by surprise.

He crossed the street without being seen by those who were inside the saloon. He stood beside the door where he could not be seen by those inside. He heard the babble of yelling, and heard Hugo Enzbarger's great voice over all the other noise. "We ought to string the bastards up. But then, maybe that's too much. How about tar an' feathers an' runnin' 'em out of town on a goddamn rail?"

Kilburn hurried crossed the street to the jail. He knocked, was admitted by Massey and quickly crossed to the gun rack. He took down a ten gauge, double-barreled shotgun. From a desk drawer he got a handful of shells loaded with buckshot. He put two in the gun and the rest in his pocket. He said, "They're talking about tar-and-feathering Tafoya and his sons. Keep the door locked, but be ready to open it quick when you see me coming back."

He stepped out into the street. Once more, the merciless heat of the midday sun hit him like a blow. He hurried toward the restaurant into which the Tafoyas had disappeared half an hour before.

He reached the restaurant and had his hand on the doorknob, when he heard the noise of shouting increase. Glancing toward the Ute Saloon, he saw men boiling out of it. This time, they left their horses tied to the rail in front of the saloon.

He went quickly into the restaurant, not knowing whether he had been seen. Jennie was behind the counter, looking white and scared. Tafoya and his two sons were sitting at the counter. They had not yet been served. Jennie had just brought their coffee.

Kilburn smiled as reassuringly as he could at Jennie. He said, "Oscar, I think you and your boys had better come with me."

"Why?"

"Enzbarger has been buying drinks for the Red Creek men. He's got them all worked up. They're coming here after you right now, and they're talking of tar and feathers and riding you on a rail."

Jennie gasped. Oscar Tafoya's face looked a little pale. His sons also looked scared, but they were defiant, too. Miguel picked up his rifle, which was leaning against the counter at his side. "Nobody's going to tar and feather me!"

Kilburn said, "Come on. Out the back door. There isn't time for argument."

Miguel said, "Pa . . ."

Oscar Tafoya's voice was sterner than Kilburn had ever heard it before. "The sheriff said there was no time for argument! We will talk about it later, but we will not talk about it now!"

Kilburn said, "Come on." He pushed the

three ahead of him into the kitchen. He glanced at Jennie. "Don't argue with him. Let them come on through if that's what they want to do."

She nodded mutely. He passed Maggie Morgan too swiftly to say anything. Then he was in the alley behind the restaurant.

He pushed ahead of the three Tafoyas. Leading them, he ran down the alley until he reached a narrow passageway between two buildings. It opened onto First Street, and he stopped at its end and peered into the street. He could see a few men standing at the corner, probably waiting to get into the restaurant.

He didn't dare wait any longer even though he knew if he and the Tafoyas crossed the street right now they would be seen. He stepped out, beckoning the Tafoyas to follow.

Immediately a yell was raised at the corner. Kilburn said, "Don't run or they might shoot. Walk across to the vacant lot behind the hotel. We can run again when we're out of sight."

The street seemed wider than it ever had before, but they reached the far side without being fired upon. Having reached the shelter of the hotel, Kilburn began to run again. The Tafoyas pounded along through the dry weeds behind him.

Beyond the livery stable, Kilburn cut hard right and burst out into Main Street between the livery stable and the jail. The mob, having pursued through the restaurant and out its back door, was just rounding the corner of First and Main.

A gun barked as Kilburn pounded on the jail door with his fist. "Dan! It's me! Open up!"

The door swung open, and the Tafoyas crowded in, Kilburn after them. Those leading the mob were only a dozen yards away when he slammed it behind him and shot the bolt.

He was soaked with sweat. He pushed back his hat and said feelingly, "Jesus! I'll be glad when all this is over with!"

Oscar asked, "When is it going to be over with?"

Kilburn shrugged, having no answer except to say, "If it would only rain! This isn't like those people. They've never done anything like this before."

Outside, Enzbarger's great voice bawled, "Kilburn!"

With the shotgun cradled in his arms, Kilburn opened the door. Enzbarger yelled, "We want the Tafoyas! We want Guthrie, too!"

"What for?"

"Never mind that. Just turn 'em over to us, and nothing will happen to you."

Kilburn said, "Hugo, Rudy is going to trial. Nothing you do is going to change that. Now go on home before somebody does something they're going to be sorry for." He could see even before the words were out that they were wasted. The men with Enzbarger were half-drunk, and they had already broken the law several times over. Words were not going to turn them back now.

He stayed there in the doorway staring at the men. Grumbling, they turned away and went across the street to the saloon. More liquor would make them more dangerous, but it would also take more time.

Kilburn backed into the jail and locked the door. He looked at Oscar Tafoya and his two sons. "Oscar, if I was you, I'd take your boys and get out of town."

The sheepman nodded reluctantly. Miguel said, "No. We have done nothing wrong. We will not be driven out."

His father said sharply, "Miguel!"

Miguel faced him defiantly. Joseph moved over to stand beside his brother. He said, "Miguel is right. Domingo lies dead, killed by Hugo Enzbarger's son. We are not going to be driven out by Enzbarger before Domingo is even in his grave."

Kilburn said, "Joseph, do what your father says. If you stay, somebody is going to get killed."

"Domingo was killed. That is all I can think right now. We will not leave."

Oscar Tafoya stared at his sons, exasperation in his face. But something else was there as well, a kind of reluctant pride. He said, "It's only for a day or two. Until things calm down. Then we'll come back, and Domingo can be laid to rest in peace."

Miguel asked fiercely, "Did he die in peace? No! He was murdered. And now, why do you think Enzbarger wants to drive us out of town? Because he thinks he can break his son out of jail, that's why."

Joseph nodded, meeting his father's angry glance defiantly. "He is right. Enzbarger is behind all this. He wants to break Rudy out of jail and let him get away."

Oscar Tafoya looked at Frank Kilburn. "Is this true?"

Kilburn nodded reluctantly. "That's the way it looks. Enzbarger is the one that's keeping them all stirred up. Right now I'd say he's trying to talk them into breaking open the jail and getting Guthrie out. Only it isn't Guthrie he's interested in. While the mob is taking Guthrie, Enzbarger will be releasing his son."

Tafoya asked, "If we stay, will we be of any help to you?"

Kilburn nodded. "You sure as hell will. I've been trying to get some of the townspeople to help but I haven't had much luck."

"Then we will stay." Tafoya smiled at his sons. They grinned back at him.

It was now midafternoon. Kilburn said, "We've got to eat and now is as good as time as any. That bunch will be busy loading up on whiskey for a while."

He didn't expect real trouble until after dark. There was a feeling of anonymity in darkness there never was in the glare of day. He said, "Come on, Dan," and went to the door. The two stepped out onto the walk, into the merciless heat of the afternoon sun.

The door closed behind him and the bolt shot home. He walked slowly toward the restaurant, with Dan Massey keeping pace.

With the Tafoyas to help, he had a better chance than he'd had before of keeping the lid on things. But with Enzbarger buying all the drinks the Red Creek men could hold and egging them on the way he was, things could blow sky-high at any time.

He glanced up at the brassy sky. Not a cloud was visible. A hot wind still blew out of the south.

Heat and helplessness did strange things to the minds of men, creating what was almost an insanity. He thought, *God, why won't it rain?*

XVIII

Jennie was standing at the restaurant window as Kilburn and Dan Massey stepped inside. Her face was pale and her eyes were scared. Kilburn said, "Jennie, I need meals for the men down at the jail. Seven in all. And two for Dan and me. We'll eat them here while you're getting the others ready."

She nodded but she didn't move. He said, "Jennie?"

She nodded again. This time she started toward the kitchen. Kilburn asked, "Nothing happened a while ago when they came through here after us, did it?"

She shook her head. He crossed the room to her, understanding that fright had all but paralyzed her thoughts. He put his arms around her and could feel her trembling. He said, "Jennie, as soon as I leave here, you go home. You and your mother both."

She found her voice. "Why? What's going to happen?"

"They may try to rush the jail."

"Can't you get help? Surely there are enough men in town to make those men go home."

He said, "I tried getting help. I didn't get enough, but I did get Dan and Sam Schell. And I've got Oscar Tafoya and his sons."

"What good will they do against thirty men?"

"Maybe some of those thirty men will come to their senses before it's too late. Go on, Jennie. Get us something to eat."

He released her. Jennie hurried toward the kitchen. He heard her talking to her mother but he couldn't make out their words.

Dan Massey sat down at the counter. Kilburn went to the window and stared down the sunbaked street. Not a soul was in sight. A dog sat in the narrow strip of shade cast by the livery barn and scratched unenthusiastically.

Kilburn turned and crossed the room. He sat down beside Dan. Jennie brought two cups of coffee from the kitchen.

Kilburn and Dan sipped their coffee silently. Its heat made sweat spring out all over Kilburn's body. It was ten minutes before Jennie brought their meal.

Kilburn ate quickly and without enjoyment. It was really too hot to eat, but he knew this might be the last meal he got today. They were finished by the time Jennie came out with the seven trays.

Kilburn took three and Dan Massey took the other four. Jennie held the door for them. Passing through it, Kilburn leaned down and kissed her lightly on the cheek. "You and your mother go home. Close the restaurant for today."

She nodded mutely, her eyes clinging almost desperately to his face. The door closed behind him. He did not look back, but he knew she was watching from the window, knew she would continue to watch until he and Massey disappeared into the jail.

Jennie did, indeed, watch until Kilburn and Massey disappeared into the jail. Then she turned, removing her apron as she did. She called, "Ma, I'm going over and see Judge Barngrover. Frank said we were to close the restaurant for today."

Maggie came from the kitchen. "You be careful."

Jennie nodded, and Maggie said, "I'll close up. After you see the judge, you go on home."

Jennie went out the door. The sun hit her like a blow. Lifting her skirts slightly, she crossed the street diagonally, heading for the judge's house.

Mrs. Barngrover answered her knock. "The judge is at the courthouse, Jennie."

Jennie nodded and hurried up the street to the courthouse. She had watched Judge Barngrover stand silently while the Red Creek men broke into the bank and seized and burned their mortgages. She had watched him stand silently by while they made a bonfire in the street out of the county clerk's record book. Jennie didn't think it was very likely that he now would take a stand. But she had to try.

Barngrover was in his courtroom, pacing back and forth. Jennie said, "Judge, the sheriff needs your help."

He frowned at her. "What do you expect me to do?"

"I should think you would know what to do."

"Frank Kilburn can handle it."

"Against a drunken mob of thirty men?"

He stared irritably at her. "Go on home, Jennie. Keep out of this."

"The way you're keeping out of it?"

He flushed and stared angrily at her. But finally he shrugged. "All right, all right. I'll go down to the depot and telegraph for men."

"What men? If the people in Guthrie

won't help their own sheriff, who do you think *will* help?"

The judge's flush deepened. "Don't you get snippety with me, young lady."

"You haven't answered me." Jennie was not ordinarily this brash, but she was terrified that Frank Kilburn was going to get hurt or even killed.

"Well, I can get men from Fort Douglass."

"That's fifty miles away."

"A special train could get them here in three hours."

"If one was available. And if the troops left right away."

Barngrover said irritably, "All I can do is ask." He took his hat off a coat tree and put it on. "I'd suggest you go home now, young lady. You're not safe on the street today."

Jennie nodded. She went out with him and watched him walk away down the street in the direction of the railroad depot. Before he reached the saloon, he crossed to the other side of the street.

Jennie walked slowly home, staying off both Main and First. Like Frank, she doubted if anything would happen until it got dark, though she had to admit they hadn't waited for dark to loot the bank and burn the county clerk's record book.

When she got home, she went upstairs immediately. From one of the closets, she got her father's old shotgun. It was a double-barreled piece, handsomely engraved. She knew where the shells for it were kept and she got them out. She took the gun out the back door and hid it, along with the shells, in the woodshed behind the house. Maybe the men in town wouldn't help Frank, but she would. This house was hardly more than a block away from the jail, and a gunshot would carry that distance easily. On Saturday nights, she could usually hear the yelling down at the Ute Saloon. She'd also hear the yelling tonight.

Going back into the house, she sat down and began to rock. Terror grew in her until it was a coldness all along her spine. She had a feeling that Frank was not going to be alive tomorrow. They'd never be married because Frank was going to die. By the time her mother arrived home from the restaurant, she was weeping almost uncontrollably.

Judge Barngrover watched the saloon out of the corner of his eye as he passed the jail. He could hear yelling over there, and he could pick out the loudest voice as that of Hugo Enzbarger, whose son was in jail charged with the murder of Oscar Tafoya's youngest son.

None of it made sense. No more than looting the bank and burning the county clerk's record book made sense. But then men who are desperate, who can see no hope, seldom do make sense. Judge Barngrover knew this from long experience on the bench.

Reaching the depot, he went inside. The telegraph key was silent. Silas Norwood sat tilted back in his swivel chair, his feet up on the desk. His eyes were closed, but the judge knew he was not asleep. His face was shiny with sweat, and his blue shirt was stained at the armpits and down the front. Barngrover said, "Silas, I want you to send a telegram."

Norwood sat up, a middle-aged, paunchy man, who had not taken time to shave today. He reached for a pad of message blanks and took a pencil from above his ear.

Barngrover said, "Send it to Colonel Benson, Fort Douglass. I want it to say, 'Request troops immediately to quell insurrection and riot here. Local law enforcement has broken down.' Sign it, 'Barngrover, County Judge.' "

Norwood went to the telegraph key and clicked the message out. He said, "It may be a while before the colonel can answer you. The telegraph wires between Junction City and the fort have been down for days.

191

The operator in Junction City will have to send a man out to the fort."

Barngrover said, "I'll be at the courthouse. Get his reply to me as soon as it comes in."

He went out. Going back, he clung to the strip of shade cast by the buildings on the south side of the street, wincing whenever he was forced to step out into the direct rays of the sun.

He didn't know for sure, of course, but he suspected that sending the telegram had been a gesture, nothing more. The railroad wasn't going to clear the tracks and send a special train to Guthrie, fifty miles away. And even if they would, Barngrover knew how slowly the Army always moved. Col. Benson would have to send a wire requesting authorization for using troops to Washington. Or to his departmental headquarters at the very least. That telegram and his answer were certain to take a lot of time. And it would probably take several hours to get the troops ready even after they were authorized.

No. Frank Kilburn was on his own. Tonight, Frank Kilburn was going to earn his pay.

The interior of the jail was probably the coolest place in town, but even in the jail,

Frank Kilburn thought, it must be over ninety degrees. Back in the cell, Guthrie, Epperson and Enzbarger growled at each other and complained to Kilburn of the heat. Only Epperson had eaten his dinner. Both Enzbarger and Guthrie had turned it down.

The trays were stacked on a table beside the door, waiting to be taken back to the restaurant. Oscar Tafoya stood at the window, looking across the street at the open doors of the saloon. The noise of shouting faintly filtered through the closed windows of the jail. Tafoya said, "Tomorrow is Domingo's funeral."

Nobody answered him. Tafoya turned. "I think we ought to talk."

Kilburn asked, "What about?"

"About what we're going to do when that mob attacks the jail."

"We don't know they're going to attack."

"No," Tafoya agreed. "We don't. But suppose they do? What are we going to do?"

Kilburn shrugged. "Hold it as long as we can, I guess." He knew what Tafoya was getting at, but he didn't want to discuss it, either with Tafoya and his sons, or with Dan Massey and Sam Schell. It was better left alone until events made delaying a decision no longer possible.

Tafoya persisted, "What do you mean, hold it as long as we can? I think we ought to decide right now how far we are going to go in defense of the prisoners."

Kilburn said, "We either defend them or we don't."

A look of annoyance crossed Tafoya's face. "You know what I mean. Are we willing to kill in their defense? Are we going to kill those men when they break into the jail?"

It was a question Kilburn had been asking himself ever since the mob had formed. He had sidestepped a decision when they attacked the bank. He had sidestepped it again when they seized and destroyed the county record book. But when they confronted him out in front of the jail tonight and threatened the lives of his prisoners, he would no longer be able to sidestep it. He'd have to make a decision and make it fast. Once made, he'd have to stick to it. Worse, he'd have to live with its consequences the rest of his life.

Tafoya was now doing only what Kilburn desperately wanted to do himself. He was trying to decide how he would meet that mob when and if it threatened to break down the door of the jail. Tafoya said, "Well?"

Kilburn said, "I can't tell the rest of you

what to do. But I'd like to know what you think you're going to do."

Tafoya said honestly, "I doubt if I can shoot into them."

Miguel stared at his father, disappointment evident in his face. He said, "Don't worry, Sheriff. I can shoot into them. And I will."

Kilburn studied Miguel, whose own self-doubt was very evident. Miguel would cave in when the time for decision came, he thought. He glanced at Joseph, who shook his head. "I don't know. I just don't know."

Kilburn glanced away. He looked at Dan Massey and then at Schell. Neither man could meet his glance. He said, "Don't worry about it. Maybe we won't have to face that decision at all."

But he knew they would. And he knew when the showdown came, Joseph would be the only one able to shoot into the mob.

He also knew what he himself would do, and he knew the basis upon which his decision had been made.

He could live with himself afterward if he killed one or more members of a mob in defense of his prisoners. But he could never live with himself if he gave his prisoners up to the demands of a lawless mob.

He said, "I think all of us had better get

some sleep, if it's possible. It's going to be a damn long night."

It would, indeed, he thought as he put his booted feet up on the desk, leaned back and closed his eyes. It would be a long night. It might even be his last.

XIX

Kilburn dozed for a while, sometimes snoring softly but waking often to listen to the growing noise coming from the Ute Saloon across the street. The afternoon waned but the heat did not decrease. Back in the cell, Epperson, having made peace with what he believed would be his fate, slept sprawled out on his back. Rudy Enzbarger paced nervously back and forth. Guthrie sat on the side of his bunk, silent and brooding, saying nothing, looking at the floor.

In the office, Dan Massey and Sam Schell sat in straight-backed chairs tilted against the wall. Both men rolled and smoked cigarettes one after the other until the room was blue with smoke. Oscar Tafoya and his two sons sat on the office couch side by side, occasionally talking together softly in Spanish, which Kilburn did not understand.

It was the longest afternoon in Kilburn's

memory, but at last the sun sank behind the western hills and shadows crept across the town. Kilburn got up as soon as they did and went to the door. He opened it, hoping for a breeze that would be cool. Only the furnace blast of the street's heat greeted him.

He stepped outside. The noise continued unabated over at the saloon. He wished he had a beer, but he didn't dare go to the saloon after it. Doing so would be asking for trouble, and he needed no more than he already had.

Turning, he called back through the door, "Dan, see if any of the prisoners need to go to the outhouse."

He heard the murmur of voices inside the jail. A few moments later all three prisoners came out, followed by Dan Massey, a shotgun cradled in his arms. Kilburn said, "Go ahead. Take them back. I'll watch from here."

Massey marched the prisoners around to the back of the jail. Kilburn stayed on watch until they returned.

Light had faded swiftly from the sky. Now the street was gray. Lights winked in the windows of the saloon. Kilburn followed Massey and the prisoners inside. He bolted the door, struck a match and lighted the lamp on his desk.

Both Massey and Schell looked scared. The trouble was, Kilburn thought, there had been too much time to think. Massey and Schell had been thinking all afternoon.

He looked at the three Tafoyas, still sitting on the office couch. Oscar Tafoya's face was almost gray. His sons looked tired, but they didn't seem to be afraid. Oscar Tafoya said, "Maybe they will go home. Maybe they will get drunk and sick, and maybe they will go home."

Kilburn nodded. "Maybe. But I wouldn't count on it." He could tell by looking at Tafoya that the man wished he could get out of this. He also knew Oscar Tafoya would never mention it. He was too conscious of his obligation to help the sheriff uphold the law. He was also aware that his sons expected it of him.

There was a knock on the door. Kilburn looked out the window before he opened it. Doc Peabody was standing on the walk.

Kilburn opened the door and Doc came in. Kilburn asked, "Find out what killed Ross?"

"Fractured skull. Caused by a blow."

"Then Ute is responsible." He thought that if he arrested Willis, he would have three men in jail charged with murder. And all in less than a week.

Doc Peabody asked, "How long do you think it'll be?"

"Before they come over here? I haven't got the slightest idea. It might happen any time. Or they might wait until the middle of the night."

"What are you going to do?"

Kilburn grinned ruefully. "Hell, Doc, I don't know. I'm going to try and avoid trouble with them if I can. But I'm not going to give up my prisoners. I knew a man once that gave a prisoner to a mob. He never got over it. He started drinking, and he died a hopeless drunk."

"You'd shoot into them?"

Kilburn nodded reluctantly. "If I had to."

Doc didn't reply, and after a moment Kilburn said, "The hell of it is, a man's liable to hold off too long. If he does, they get his prisoner anyway. But if he doesn't hold off and kills somebody, then he's got to spend the rest of his life wondering if he shot too soon. Don't seem like a man can win, no matter what he does."

He sat down at his desk and lifted his scarred boots to its top. Doc shuffled to the only other chair in the room, a dilapidated wicker rocker. It creaked when he sat down and creaked monotonously as he rocked.

When it was completely dark outside, Kilburn lighted another lamp. He took it back into the corridor opposite the cell and placed it on a shelf.

He sat down at his desk again. The clock ticked monotonously. Doc Peabody's rocker squeaked in rhythm with the clock.

The hours passed. At last, a surge of noise from across the street brought Kilburn to his feet. He went to the window and peered outside.

Massey, Schell, the Tafoyas and Doc Peabody crowded the window, also looking out. The saloon across the street disgorged a crowd of men. Hugo Enzbarger and his two sons led the others across the street. Hugo was yelling, but Kilburn could not make out his words.

Not that he needed to. He knew what Hugo was saying to them. He stepped away from the window. He picked up the shotgun he had loaded earlier. He checked its loads by breaking the action and closed it with a snap.

Outside, Enzbarger yelled, "Kilburn, open up! We've come for one of your prisoners!"

Kilburn went to the door. He looked at Dan. "Bolt it behind me but stand by. I might have to come in quick."

He unbolted the door and stepped outside. He heard the bolt shoot home behind him.

He had never felt more alone. He held the shotgun cradled in his arms, a thumb on one of the hammers. He looked at Enzbarger. "Which of the prisoners do you want?"

"Guthrie. Who else? And we want them damn sheepmen, too."

Kilburn said, "No. I'm not giving up anyone."

"We'll take 'em. We'll take 'em, and if you stand in our way . . ."

Kilburn looked beyond him at the men who lived along Red Creek. They were a wild-looking bunch, in various stages of drunkenness. All were armed, most with revolvers, some with rifles, a couple with shotguns, probably loaded with birdshot rather than with buck. Kilburn yelled, "All of you go home. So far, all you've done is destroy property. But you're talking about murder, now. If you take Guthrie and the Tafoyas, and if anything happens to them, then every one of you is as guilty as the one who pulls the trggger or puts the rope on them."

He could see that his words had partially sobered some of them. Looking around, Hugo Enzbarger saw that, too. He bawled,

"Don't listen to the son-of-a-bitch! I told you he'd try to talk you out of it! I say we've come this far, let's go all the way! They ain't going to bring thirty of us to trial."

Enzbarger's sons chimed in, agreeing with him. Kilburn looked for Hattie Pomeroy in the crowd without finding her. He supposed she had gone home.

Enzbarger and his sons stood in the middle of the street. The others who were massed behind Enzbarger moved forward now, slowly, so that the men behind him would keep up. He shouted, "Stand aside, Kilburn, or somebody's going to get hurt."

All of them were yelling now, yelling to still the doubts that lingered in their minds. And there was a contagious quality to their yelling that made them yell louder all the time.

Kilburn knew it was too late now to stop them, too late to turn them back with words. Raising the shotgun muzzle, he thumbed the hammer back and squeezed the trigger off.

The shotgun's roar rolled along the street, echoing back from buildings and, moments later, from the bluff to the east of town. It froze Enzbarger and his sons in their tracks. It made the rest of the mob take an involuntary backward step. Kilburn swiftly broke the action of the gun and, catching the live shell as it ejected reinserted it, along with a live cartridge to replace the fired one, which lay smoked at his feet

The shouting had momentarily stilled following the shotgun blast. In the silence, Kilburn's voice was cold, "Hugo, the next one is going to cut you in two." He shifted the gun so that it pointed straight at Enzbarger. A murmur began among the men behind Enzbarger. They shifted, those behind Enzbarger moving away to right and left so that scattering buckshot would not hit them if it missed Enzbarger.

For an instant, Kilburn thought that he had won. But Enzbarger's stake in this was too great for him to back away. His son's life was at stake. Growling deep in his throat, he moved toward Kilburn again.

Kilburn tightened his finger on the trigger, knowing even as he did that if he shot the mob would surge forward and overwhelm him before he could get inside. He hesitated, and at the last instant knew he could not kill Enzbarger. Not yet at least. Not until there was certainty that if he did not the mob would get his prisoners.

He rammed the shotgun butt against the door as a signal and heard the bolt withdrawn. He leaped backward through the door, slamming it and throwing his weight against it as Dan Massey shot the bolt.

The bolt was scarcely home before Enzbarger's great bulk hit the door, rattling it despite its weight. Kilburn thought, *My God, but that was close!* as he eased the hammer of the shotgun down, then broke the action to prevent the gun from firing accidentally.

Outside, a frustrated roar went up, and something hammered against the door. Kilburn said, "Blow out the lamps."

There was a quick flurry of movement in the office and cell corridor. The room went dark. Kilburn said, "Get down on the floor. Everyone. Next thing they'll do is shoot through the windows and the door."

He dropped to the floor, keeping his hold on the shotgun. Almost instantly bullets riddled the door, showering those inside with splinters torn out of it. Glass tinkled to the floor as bullets broke both windows simultaneously.

After that, there was a moment's silence. Kilburn asked, "Anybody want to leave?"

Nobody replied. Kilburn said, "No use in being stupid. Dan, I want you and Sam to go. They'll let you through. And I want you to leave, too, Doc."

Nobody answered. Kilburn said impatiently, "Dan? Sam?"

Sam Schell said, "Well, if you're sure we can't do you any good."

"You can't. Doc?"

"I'll stay if you want me to."

"I don't."

"What about Oscar and his boys?"

"They can leave if they want. But I think they'll be better off in here." He turned his head to look back toward the cell. "Guthrie, you can go with them if you want."

"No thanks. I'll stay right here." Guthrie's voice was dry. If he was afraid, it wasn't noticeable in his tone of voice.

Kilburn raised his head. "Enzbarger?" he yelled.

Outside, Hugo Enzbarger shouted back, "What?"

"Dan and Sam and Doc Peabody are coming out."

Enzbarger roared, "Hold your fire, boys. We ain't got anything against them three."

Kilburn stood up. He crossed the room and unbolted the door. "Come on."

He opened the door only enough to permit the three to squeeze their bodies through. Then he closed and bolted it again.

Outside, the mob cheered Dan and Sam and Doc Peabody. The cheering was very brief. Then Kilburn heard Enzbarger's voice again. "Some of you go on down to the depot and get a railroad tie!"

The railroad tie was for a battering ram. In a couple of blows it would demolish the door of the jail.

It suddenly struck Kilburn that he was going to die. There was no way out of it. He, and Guthrie and the Tafoyas were going to die. Only Epperson and Rudy Enzbarger were going to walk out of the jail alive.

XX

Some of the men in the street took the opportunity to return to the saloon. They emerged, carrying bottles in their hands.

Darkness had not brought relief from the heat. It seemed, in fact, even more oppressive than it had by day. A yell broke from the throats of the mob and, peering out, Kilburn saw four men come trotting up the street carrying a railroad tie, black with creosote.

Others joined them, and all hurried toward the jail. Kilburn could have fired through the window but he did not. He retreated across the office and stood in front of the cell, the shotgun in his hands. Tafoya and his two sons joined him, nervously fingering their guns. Kilburn said, "I'd suggest you put down your guns. They're coming in. I can't stop them. If you have guns in your hands, you're going to get killed."

Oscar Tafoya put down his gun, leaning it against the wall. His sons looked at him, then at Kilburn, baffled anger and frustration in their faces. Then, as though realizing they had no other choice, they crossed to the desk and put their guns on it. Kilburn motioned them to the far side of the room. They shuffled there reluctantly.

The first blow of the railroad tie rattled the door thunderously and loosened the doorjamb where the hinges were. They'd come in next time, he thought, and thumbed one hammer of the shotgun back. Now, at this last instant, he knew what he was going to do. He would not surrender, even if they gave him a chance. He would fire when Enzbarger came through the door because only by killing Enzbarger could he hope to stop the mob.

The second blow left the door hanging from one hinge. Now Kilburn could see the faces of the men in the street, eerily illuminated by lanterns carried by a few of them. The ram struck again, this time flinging the shattered door halfway across the room.

Those carrying the ram pulled back precipitously, dropping the tie, leaving it lying half in, half out of the door. Others came crowding into the breach, guns ready in their hands, mob insanity in their eyes. Kilburn stared, appalled by what he saw. These were not men he knew. There were strangers, bent on violence and death.

His finger was curled around the trigger of the shotgun. His thumb was on the hammer that controlled barrel number two. And then, flinging the others aside recklessly, Hugo Enzbarger came plunging into the jail.

He had a revolver in his hand. Its hammer was thumbed back. The muzzle swept the room, passed over the Tafoyas and found Kilburn against the bars of the cell.

Enzbarger hesitated a fraction of a second while his glance went past the sheriff, looking for Rudy to be sure he was not in the line of fire. In that instant, Kilburn pulled the trigger of his gun.

The roar of the ten gauge in this confined area was awe-inspiring. Smoke from the muzzle blast rolled across the room, struck the front wall and followed it to the ceiling, then rolled back along the ceiling toward the place where Kilburn stood.

Hugo Enzbarger was literally cut in two. He was driven back against his sons, against those behind the two. His blood and shredded entrails drenched them so that it was impossible to tell who had been hit by the spreading charge and who had not. Kilburn roared, "Get out of here, or by God, I'll let you have the other one!"

Through the clearing smoke he saw Karl and Sam, Hugo's sons, standing in the door. Karl had a rifle and it was pointing straight at him. He thumbed back the hammer of the ten gauge and let go the second blast.

The roar of this one was as terrifying as the first had been. Once more smoke billowed across the room.

Powdersmoke from the two shotgun blasts had completely filled the room. Kilburn's eyes burned, and he began to cough. He fumbled frantically in his pocket for two more shells. With violently trembling fingers, he tried to stuff them into the gun. He had never killed a man before. He had never seen one literally cut in two by a shotgun blast. He felt as if, even in peril, he was going to be sick.

Hugo Enzbarger lay sprawled against the blood-soaked wall. Karl lay slumped in the doorway opening, over the creosoted railroad tie. Sam, the last of the three, had the blood of his brother and of his father on his face and chest. He was also wounded, but not mortally. With a sound like that of a charging animal, he came across the room toward Kilburn, gun forgotten, hands outstretched as if he wanted to tear Kilburn apart with them.

Behind Sam came the surging mob. Sam struck Kilburn and slammed him against the bars of the cell. His hand closed on Kilburn's throat.

Something struck Kilburn's head. It stunned him but didn't knock him out. Sam Enzbarger's tightening hands cut off the air from his lungs. He writhed and struggled, but others were now helping Sam. And suddenly a gun stock slammed against the side of Kilburn's head. He descended into blackness and knew no more.

When he regained consciousness, he was no longer at the jail. He was out beneath the sky, in the bed of Red Creek, beneath a towering cottonwood.

Torches and lanterns illuminated the eerie scene. There were angry voices and drunken ones. Nooses fashioned from lariats dangled from a nearly horizontal limb. Five of them. One for each of the Tafoyas, he thought. One for Guthrie. One for him.

He was yanked unceremoniously to his feet. His head whirled and ached ferociously. Five frightened horses were led beneath the limb. Rudy Enzbarger roared at the men to hoist the victims on their backs.

Kilburn heard the shouts as if from a distance. He saw the distorted faces of the men who were going to kill him. He seemed to be looking through the wavy glass of a bottle. He felt a strangeness that he attributed to his injury. But it was not his injury. There was an electric feeling in the air, a stillness not usual.

A sudden breath of air made the lanterns flicker. Guthrie, struggling in spite of his tied hands and feet, was hoisted to a horse, held there while a mounted man put the noose over his head and drew it tight. Kicking and struggling, Oscar Tafoya was boosted onto the second horse.

The air stirred again, the breeze quickening. Miraculously the breath of air was cool. And then, as if the Almighty was furious at what he saw, a bolt of lightning crackled from the sky, striking the cottonwood, stripping bark from its gigantic trunk.

Stunned, men fell to the ground. Horses galloped away into the night, nickering shrilly in their fear. Guthrie and Oscar Tafoya lay beneath the limb, the nooses still around their necks, unhurt. The ends of the ropes had never been secured.

And now, thunder from the awful lightning

bolt echoed back from the surrounding bluffs. And the rain came down, at first in great drops that raised puffs of dust from the parched land, then in smaller drops that came in blowing sheets, drenching men and horses instantly.

More lightning bolts slashed across the darkened sky, to be followed by sonorous rolls of thunder that echoed and reechoed across the swimming land.

In the flickering lantern light, the men of Red Creek lifted their streaming faces to the sky. They let the rain beat against them, as if this were some kind of cleansing ritual.

Having done so, they looked at each other and at the men they had intended to kill. Then, one by one, they shuffled ashamedly away, heads down, faces averted. Those who could find their horses rode away toward home. Those who could not ride, walked. In minutes, only the Tafoyas, Guthrie and Kilburn remained beneath the cottonwood.

Kilburn turned toward town, rubbing the lump on the side of his head where the gun stock had struck. He was dizzy and sick, but he was alive.

Lightning flashed again. In its white glare he saw a girl standing at the clearing's edge, a shotgun in her hands.

Jennie Morgan, he thought, as he saw her

drop the gun and run toward him. He stopped and held out his arms, and an instant later she ran into them.

They stood there in the driving rain for a long, long time, each content to feel that the other was alive.

It was Kilburn who at last pulled back. "How long have you been standing there?" he asked.

"Since they brought you here."

"Would you have used the gun?"

Her voice, when it came, was firm with anger and outrage. "You're damned right I would. The minute they tried to hoist you on a horse."

Kilburn grinned. With his arm around her waist, he walked toward town, heedless of the rain, heedless of the slippery mud underfoot. Tomorrow he could get back to the business of being sheriff again. By recapturing Enzbarger and Epperson.

But for tonight, it was enough that the insanity had gone. And tomorrow the yellow sky would be blue again.

ABOUT THE AUTHOR

Lewis B. Patten wrote more than ninety Western novels in thirty years and three of them won Spur Awards from the Western Writers of America and the author himself the Golden Saddleman Award. Indeed, this highlights the most remarkable aspect of his work: not that there is so much of it, but that so much of it is so fine. Patten was born in Denver, Colorado, and served in the U.S. Navy 1933–1937. He was educated at the University of Denver during the war years and became an auditor for the Colorado Department of Revenue during the 1940s. It was in this period that he began contributing significantly to Western pulp magazines, fiction that was from the beginning fresh and unique and revealed Patten's lifelong concern with the sociological and psychological affects of group psychology on the frontier. He became a professional writer at the time of his first novel, *Mas-*

sacre at White River (1952). The dominant theme in much of his fiction is the notion of justice, and its opposite, injustice. In his first novel it has to do with exploitation of the Ute Indians, but as he matured as a writer he explored this theme with significant and poignant detail in small towns throughout the early West. Crimes, such as rape or lynching, were often at the centre of his stories. When the values embodied in these small towns are examined closely, they are found to be wanting. Conformity is always easier than taking a stand. Yet, in Patten's view of the American West, there is usually a man or a woman who refuses to conform. Among his finest titles, always a difficult choice, surely are *A Killing at Kiowa* (1972), *Ride a Crooked Trail* (1976), and his many fine contributions to Doubleday's Double D series, including *Villa's Rifles* (1977), *The Law at Cottonwood* (1978), and *Death Rides a Black Horse* (1978). His most recent books are *Tincup in the Storm Country* (1996), *Trail to Vicksburg* (1997), *Death Rides the Denver Stage* (1999), and *The Woman at Ox-Yoke* (2000).

We hope you have enjoyed this Large Print book. Other Thorndike, Wheeler, and Chivers Press Large Print books are available at your library or directly from the publishers.

For information about current and upcoming titles, please call or write, without obligation, to:

Publisher
Thorndike Press
295 Kennedy Memorial Drive
Waterville, ME 04901
Tel. (800) 223-1244

or visit our Web site at:

www.gale.com/thorndike
www.gale.com/wheeler

OR

Chivers Large Print
published by BBC Audiobooks Ltd
St James House, The Square
Lower Bristol Road
Bath BA2 3SB
England
Tel. +44(0) 800 136919
email: bbcaudiobooks@bbc.co.uk
www.bbcaudiobooks.co.uk

All our Large Print titles are designed for easy reading, and all our books are made to last.